FROM FEAR TO ETERNITY

book five of the matchmaker mysteries series

elise sax

Cover design: Sprinkles On Top Studios
Edited by: Novel Needs
Formatted by: Jesse Kimmel-Freeman

Printed in the United States of America

elisesax.com
elisesax@gmail.com
https://bit.ly/2PzAhRx
https://www.facebook.com/ei.sax.9

For Susan, my pusher....

ALSO BY ELISE SAX

Matchmaker Mysteries Series

Matchmaking Advice from Your
Grandma Zelda
Road to Matchmaker
An Affair to Dismember
Citizen Pain
The Wizards of Saws
Field of Screams

From Fear to Eternity
West Side Gory
Scareplane
It Happened One Fright
The Big Kill
It's a Wonderful Knife
Ship of Ghouls

Goodnight Mysteries Series

Die Noon
A Doom with a View
Jurassic Dark
Coal Miner's Slaughter
Wuthering Frights

Agatha Bright Mysteries Series

The Fear Hunter
Some Like It Shot
Fright Club
Beast of Eden
Creepy Hollow

Matchmaker Marriage Mysteries

Gored of the Rings
Slay Misty for Me
Scar Wars
Die Charred
Spawn with the Wind

Partners in Crime Series

Partners in Crime
Conspiracy in Crime
Divided in Crime
Surrender in Crime

Operation Billionaire Trilogy

How to Marry a Billionaire
How to Marry Another Billionaire
How to Marry the Last Billionaire on Earth

Five Wishes Series

Going Down
Man Candy
Hot Wired
Just Sacked
Wicked Ride
Five Wishes Series

Three More Wishes Series

Blown Away
Inn & Out
Quick Bang
Three More Wishes Series

Standalone Books

Forever Now
Bounty
Switched
Delivery Happiness

CHAPTER 1

I get a lot of matches. People come to me from all over the world. Did you know that, bubeleh? One time I even got a lovely gentleman from the North Pole. Business is good. I can't complain. But did you know that a lot of people want to come to me, but they're afraid? Fear is a strong enemy of love. What are they afraid of, you might ask. That they're not beautiful enough. That they're not smart enough. That they're not rich enough. That they're not lovable enough. But the number one biggest fear is that they're too old. Too old for love…have you ever heard of such mishegas? Yes, I bet you have. Something happens to our thinking as we get closer to our final days. Instead of visualizing ourselves as vessels full of a lifetime's worth of wisdom, kindness, beauty, and love, we see ourselves as reaching our "use by" date. We picture the last of our wisdom, kindness, beauty, and love draining out of ourselves, just like our supply of estrogen and skin elasticity until there's gornisht. Bupkes. These matches see themselves as worthless bags of skin never

elise sax

to feel again the euphoria of the first sparks of passion with a new love. I don't blame them too much. After all, a sixty-year old tuchus isn't usually a thing of beauty. But that doesn't mean that that tuchus doesn't deserve as much love as a twenty-year old tuchus. How to alleviate your potential matches' fears, you might ask? The proof is in the pudding, dolly. Don't wait for them to ask. Push them off the cliff and match them, even if they're too scared to ask. Go to them. Match their tuchus.

Lesson 76, Matchmaking Advice from Your Grandma Zelda

My grandmother thought I shared her gift for knowing things that couldn't be known, but that Tuesday, I had no idea that old man Dwight Foyle was about to be murdered and that I was going to find his body…as usual. Maybe Grandma was right, and I did have a third eye waiting to make its appearance, but for now, it was being distracted by Spencer.

Oh, Spencer.

He smelled like really expensive sex. Like a young Hugh Jackman-- but much better looking-- mixed with kajillion-dollar men's cologne, mixed with a testosterone supplement that the EPA would have listed as one of the most dangerous substances on earth, mixed with a whole bunch of holy moly.

Gobs of holy moly.

Massive quantities of holy moly.

2

"Holy moly." I moaned, as his hands roamed my naked body searching for my erogenous zones. He found them all. "This is so good." I moaned again. It was good, and I knew it was going to get better. After all, we had only just started. We were naked, slick with sweat, our limbs intertwined, rolling around on the floor of the National Museum of Natural History as tour groups of tourists walked by, enjoying the dinosaur display.

Spencer looked deeply into my eyes. "Bubeleh, you want Danish or bagels for breakfast?" he asked. "I got prune Danish and pumpernickel bagels. I hear that pumpernickel is very good to keep you regular. But prune is gangbusters for a speedy bowel. How's your pooping these days?"

"Huh?" I asked the naked, muscly Spencer.

His blue eyes were dark with passion. "Your poop. How's your poop?"

"Excuse me?"

"Dolly, did you hear me?" Spencer asked.

His gorgeous face shimmered and then faded away. I grabbed for him, but he was gone. Disappeared. So was I. I was no longer naked in the Natural History Museum, no longer getting it on with the man who was supposedly in my life.

Instead, I was waking up in my bed in my grandmother's house. Speaking of Grandma, her ancient, slack

3

face was hanging over me, and she tugged at my pajama sleeve. Her hair was covered in rollers, and she was wearing her favorite blue housedress. "Well, bubeleh?" she demanded. "Danish or pumpernickel bagel? Hey, I got a good idea. Why don't we do both? I think we're going to need our strength today. We could carbo load like marathon runners."

I rubbed my eyes. "I was dreaming," I said.

She nodded. "Boy, were you dreaming. Porno dreaming. If you don't seal the deal with Spencer, you're going to blow up."

She was right. It had been two weeks since Spencer and I sort of committed ourselves to a relationship with each other. I had inadvertently said the "L" word, but when it was his turn, he sort of choked on his tongue. I hadn't seen much of him since. I didn't know if he was hiding from me or if I was hiding from him. In any case, it had been a quiet two weeks. My body was getting impatient. My grandmother was right; I was going to blow up any minute.

"I'm not going to blow up," I said, pulling the covers up under my chin. "We're just taking it slow." I could see my breath as it hit the cold air. "Grandma, it's freezing in here."

"Cold makes you sleep better. But you can get up now. I turned on the furnace. It'll be toasty in no time. We got the *New Year, New Love* meeting in an hour."

That meant I didn't have a lot of time to get my prunes and pumpernickels in me before Grandma's house was invaded by the desperate and lonely. My grandmother insisted that the cold might make you sleep better, but it was terrible for finding love. There were a whole lot of miserable people wearing long underwear in our town of Cannes, California, during this frigid January. Hopefully, the *New Year, New Love* meeting would help match up a few of them. I had moved in with my grandmother eight months before to help her with her matchmaking business. It was a steep learning curve. Grandma had a way of matching people with an almost magical gift. She assured me that I had the gift, too, but there was little evidence of it so far.

I wrapped my blanket around me and padded my way to the bathroom. I scratched a place on my arm, which was raised in an angry welt. Despite the cold January, we were getting an influx of mosquitoes. Every morning for the past week, I had been getting up with new bites on my body. It was like the mosquitoes were confused about what season it was, or they had decided to spend the winter in Grandmother's large Victorian house.

After my shower, I put calamine lotion on my bites and decided to make an effort to look the part for the day. Just as Spencer and I had sort of decided to be a couple, I had sort of decided to finally be a real matchmaker, once and for all. A professional. So, this morning I made a point to put on professional makeup and professional clothes and put my hair back in a professional ponytail. "Not bad," I told my reflection in the mirror. I looked respectable in my black turtleneck, dark green skirt, and black boots.

Downstairs, I smelled the coffee brewing. I found Grandma in the kitchen. She had stuffed her ample body into a Stella McCartney-knockoff beige power suit. Her hair was teased into submission, and she was still wearing her plastic slippers, which clacked on the linoleum when she walked around the kitchen.

"Grab the milk out of the refrigerator, Gladie," she told me.

I took out the milk and the cream cheese. The table was already set, and I picked up one of the plates as the toaster oven dinged with our pumpernickel bagels. I sat down across from Grandma, and tossed one of the bagels onto her plate. She poured coffee into a "Don't Mess With Texas" mug that she must have gotten as a gift because my grandmother never left her property line.

"Good coffee," I commented, taking a sip.

"What a day it's going to be!" she exclaimed, scratching at a mosquito bite on her neck.

"It is?" I asked, concerned. The past two weeks had been quiet, and I didn't want to ramp up any excitement in my life.

Not after my December, which had been packed with dead people and things exploding.

"You should probably eat double. Get your strength up."

I scratched at a mosquito bite on my leg. "I'm not sure I have any more strength." But I did as she told me and ate double. It was always a mistake not to listen to my grandmother. She had a way of knowing things that couldn't be known.

Just as she took the first bite of her second Danish, she froze in place. Her eyes fixed at the air above my head, and I looked to see what she was staring at. There was nothing there.

"What is it? Are you okay?" I asked.

Her face was a picture of fear. "Someone's here who shouldn't be here."

That could have meant a good hundred people. Grandma's house was the Grand Central of the town. People came and went every day. But this was different, according to my grandmother. In defense against the unknown intruder, I grabbed my butter knife with a smear of cream cheese on it. "Should I call 911?"

She blinked. "Our home has been invaded, Gladie. Something's definitely not right."

My instinct was to run like crazy, but Grandma insisted that we search the house for the unseen invader. She stood behind me and my cream-cheese smeared butter knife as we walked from one room to the next, investigating every closet and under every bed. But we found no one.

"Maybe your radar's off," I said when we reached the downstairs, again.

She thought about that a moment. "No, I'm seeing pretty clearly today. I wish I could get a handle on the invader, though. That's a bit fuzzy."

The front door opened, and a parade of women of all shapes and ages paraded in. They were repeat offenders, women who had more problems in the love arena than the average person. But my grandmother was eternally optimistic that their matches were out there somewhere. She had created the *New Year, New Love* meeting specifically for them to give them a boost for the year. Without being instructed, the group set up folding chairs in the parlor. They laid out cookies and a big pot of coffee and sat down, chatting among themselves.

"Okay, bubeleh, let's get cracking," Grandma told me.

I took a seat next to Grandma, and she nodded toward me to begin. Being responsible for other people's lives got me really nervous and I wondered if I would ever get used to it. Despite sweat breaking out on my upper lip and under my arms, I knew I'd have to soldier on. Having my grandmother with me helped. She was the backup that I needed because I knew she wouldn't let me fail while she was around. I smiled back at her, giving her a sign that I was fully on board as a professional matchmaker. She smiled back and crossed her legs. I noticed then that her heels had formed a thick crust. Normally, my grandmother was very concerned about her upkeep. Every Monday, Bird Gonzalez, the local hairdresser, would visit and give my grandmother a head-to-toe tune-up. Come to think of it, Bird hadn't come this week, which was odd. Usually, nothing came between Bird and her clients. Crusty heels or gray roots in town was bad advertising for Bird. I wondered what was wrong, and if Bird was okay.

"I'm fifty-two years old," Darlene Scholz complained. "I've already given up on my ovaries, but soon I'm going to have to give up on my vagina. You know what I mean?"

I had no idea what she meant. I shot a panicked glance at my grandmother. "Your hoo-ha has got years before it gives up the ghost," Grandma told Darlene, reassuringly.

Darlene didn't look totally convinced. I got the impression that she gave her vagina a lot of thought and knew something that we didn't know. I didn't give my vagina any thought at all, and now I was wondering if I should have. How much thought should women give to their vaginas? The fact that I didn't know made me doubt myself as a matchmaker, again.

Grandma patted my knee. "You're doing fine, Gladie," she said.

"Even with the bad weather, we need to get out and show ourselves," I began. "January is a bummer with the weather and short days. So, get out there and participate in the town's events."

"I'm allergic to the cold," Christine Lansberg interrupted. "And I can't do anything involving hot cider or hot chocolate. It throws off my numbers."

I didn't know what she meant by numbers. Did hot chocolate have a number? I shot Grandma another desperate look, and she signaled to the binder on the coffee table. I picked it up and quickly searched for Christine in it. Grandma's notes said that Christine needed a man who liked quilting and who knew how to use an EpiPen. My forehead broke out into layer of sweat.

Then it hit me. "You're right, Christine. That's why I think you should visit Henrietta's Notions." Henrietta's son had just come back from Afghanistan, where he served as a medic. He had potential as a great match. Grandma gave me an approving nod.

I was pumped up with self-confidence. This matchmaking business wasn't as hard as I thought. Maybe I really did have the gift.

The meeting went on for about another twenty minutes before we stopped for a cookie break. I hadn't had any more brainstorms, but Grandma seemed to know where three of the women should go to find their forever loves. It was all going smoothly until the front door opened and the sound of men's boots echoed through the house, stampeding like Clydesdales at the start of a Budweiser commercial.

"Oh, dear," Grandma breathed.

"What the hell?" Darlene shrieked.

I don't know why, but I shut my eyes tight. Maybe it was some sort of survival instinct.

"Save our town's good name!" a man yelled from the entranceway. I kept my eyes closed, but I could hear the *New Year, New Love* participants get up and move around. Fools. They wanted to see what the action was, but I had experience with action, and it never turned out well. I wanted nothing to do with it. Fool me once, okay. Fool me a dozen times, and…well, I had no intention of getting involved, no matter what it was. I had moved into a crazy town full of crazy characters. Normally, I got sucked into the craziness, which made me crazy, and occasionally put me in the hospital, but now I needed a moment to just be normal. Was that so much to ask?

Yes. Yes, it was.

"We're going to have truth this year, no matter what!" another man yelled. I recognized his voice. It was Jose, my grandmother's gardener. Usually he was very mild-mannered, but now he was spitting mad. He had worked with Grandma to create her prize-winning roses and crossed himself a lot around her, probably because he believed that she was a witch.

"Get that pickaxe away from my face!" another man yelled. "You want some of my axe?"

"I dare you!"

"I'll pound you one, head-in-the-sand moron!"

"Communist!"

I opened my eyes. The women of the meeting had shuffled out of the room, and Grandma was still sitting next to me, shaking her head, like she was disappointed that girls were wearing their skirts too short this year.

"You interrupted our meeting!" I heard Darlene yell at the men in the entranceway. "Now what am I going to do about my vagina?"

That seemed to quiet down whatever argument they were having. "Grandma, do you ever think of retirement?" I asked.

"Sometimes I think about becoming a welder, but I don't like heights."

She got up and walked into the other room. Reluctantly, I followed her out. The entranceway was crammed with the single women and five men armed with pickaxes and other tools that they were wielding like weapons. It would have been a great matchmaking opportunity normally, but the single women didn't look interested in the men. That was probably because the men were dressed as 19th century, filthy gold miners, and they were giving off an authentic old-timey smell, not to mention that they were wild-eyed, fighting mad, and ready for hand-to-hand combat.

"Zelda, we came here because you got to help us work this out," one of the men implored my grandmother.

"Certainly, Ralph. How can I help?"

"Jose here is rebelling against tradition. We're in a crisis that could bring down this town."

The women gasped. I sniggered and put my hand over my mouth. It would take a lot to bring down the town. We had already had a cult invasion, a flying donkey, and body parts in the freezer section of Walley's. And the town was still intact.

"Our tradition has been wrong all these years, Zelda," Jose said. Ralph threw his pickaxe on his shoulder like one of Snow White's dwarfs and huffed. Another man nodded in agreement with Jose. It was like the civil war all over again.

"I thought the gold mine was closed," I said. It had just

dawned on me that the mine had closed down over one hundred years ago. Cannes was a small mountain town east of San Diego. It had been founded with the discovery of gold in the middle of the 1800's, but the gold ran out pretty quickly, and now it was just a tourist town, filled with pie shops and antique stores.

"Of course it's closed," Ralph said, annoyed.

"Every January, the town puts on a historical play. It's been the same play since as far back as I can remember." Grandma explained. As far back as she could remember was a long time. "I'm guessing you're having creative disagreements this year?" she asked Jose.

It was my first January in Cannes since I was a little girl. I didn't remember the play at all.

"Jose and his cabal want to change the soul of this town!" one of the men shouted and shook his pickaxe.

"Fascist!"

"Lenin-loving Stalin!"

"These are not creative disagreements, Zelda," Jose said. "It's about the truth. The real, dark history of our town."

Time seemed to stand still, and there wasn't a sound in the room. We seemed to stop breathing, while we waited to hear what the "real, dark history of our town" was.

Jose opened his mouth, ready to reveal all, when another woman and man stepped through the front doorway, interrupting him.

It was like Grandma's entranceway had become the vortex for the town, the whirlpool where everyone came to drown, or at least to voice their discontent. The woman looked slightly familiar. She was mousy, in a long skirt, stretched out cardigan, and a long wool coat. The man was Andy Griffith.

"Uh," I said.

"Liar!" the mousy woman shouted and pointed at me. I looked behind me to see who she was shouting at. Nope, nobody there. She and Andy Griffith pushed their way past everyone to get into my face. "Liar! Fraud! Phony!"

"Is this part of the meeting?" one of the matches asked. "Like a show?"

"How did you get Andy Griffith for an appearance?" Darlene asked.

"I thought he was dead," Ralph said.

"It's not Andy Griffith," Grandma explained. "That's Gordon Zorro."

"Andy Griffith is Zorro?" I asked.

"He sure looks like Andy Griffith," Darlene said.

"Whistle your theme song," a man with a pickaxe demanded.

Andy Griffith or Zorro or whoever he was waved a paper in the air. "Gladie Burger, you're being served."

For a few seconds, I thought he was delivering pizza or Chinese food. Grandma caught on more quickly and retrieved the paper from his hand.

"You told me that I was going to fall in love, and I didn't," the woman screeched, her finger hanging in the air, pointing at me. All heads turned toward me…the matches and the costumed townspeople.

"I'm sorry?" I said like a question. "Do I know you?"

It was the wrong thing to say. Her eyes got huge, and she began to pant like a Chihuahua, trying—I assume--to find the right words to express her outrage.

"Maybe I know you," I said to pacify her, actually she did look familiar to me. Grandma remembered every name and face of every person that she met or saw a picture of, but I was terrible with names and faces, which was just one more sign that I probably didn't have my grandmother's gift for this business.

"Fionnula Jericho," Grandma said, gently taking her hand in hers. "What can we do for you?"

Fionnula Jericho. Fionnula Jericho. The name was

familiar, too. Oh! "Fionnula Jericho!" I cried. "Of course. You were at Romance for the Holidays. I remember you." She had been dressed pretty much the same as she was now at the meeting a couple weeks before, and instead of angry, she had been depressed. The rest was fuzzy. I remembered telling her something about falling in love, but that was it.

"You told me that I would fall in love! You're a fraud! I'm not going to rest until everyone knows it and I take every penny you have."

"I have like three pennies," I said.

"Fraud! Phony! Come on, lawyer," she said, tugging on the arm of the Andy Griffith-lookalike.

"Bye y'all," he called, and they walked out.

"Was that part of the show?" one of the matches asked.

"Are you sure that wasn't Andy? He even sounded like him," Ralph said.

My grandmother handed me the paper. I blinked twice and read through it three times because I couldn't believe my eyes. According to the paper, Fionnula Jericho was suing me for eight-hundred-thousand dollars, and Gordon Zorro was her lawyer.

"Eight hundred…eight hundred…" I hyperventilated.

"Put your hands up, bubeleh."

I put my hands up, letting the subpoena float to the floor. "Eight hundred…"

One of the men whistled. "That's a lot of clams."

"What did she do to get sued for eight-hundred-thousand, Zelda?" Darlene asked.

"She must have poisoned her dog or burned her with hot coffee. Those are big lawsuits," a man commented.

A match nodded. "Yep. Saw that on Judge Judy. I'm no expert, but it doesn't look good for you."

"It doesn't look good," I repeated, my voice hitching up like I had sucked helium. "It doesn't look good!"

"If Fionnula has Gordon Zorro, you can't mess around," Grandma said seriously.

"I can't mess around," I repeated. "Eight hundred…Eight hundred…"

"You're going to have to hire Cannes's second-biggest shark," she told me.

"Second-biggest shark? Why not the first biggest shark?"

Grandma shook her head. "Cannes's biggest shark is Gordon Zorro. So, you'll have to hire number two. John Wayne."

"John Wayne? Andy Griffith against John Wayne?"

"Don't be ridiculous. It's Zorro against John Wayne. Go now. John Wayne has a slot available until twelve o'clock. And don't stare at his face."

I nodded. "Twelve o'clock. No face."

The eight hundred thousand number had me in a state of shock. I knew that my grandmother was speaking to me, but I couldn't understand a lot of the words. I started to push my way through the crowd to visit the second biggest shark.

"Cannes police department," a gruff, authoritarian voice bellowed at the front door, stopping me in my tracks. I knew that voice. Usually it was chastising me for something or trying to get into my Spanx, but it was still the same voice.

Spencer Bolton, the police chief and my maybe, sort of, oh-who-knows boyfriend was pushing his way into the bursting-out-of-the-seams entranceway. He pushed past the single women and pickaxe-bearing men until he spotted me.

"Are you kidding me?" he demanded.

CHAPTER 2

A matchmaker's life is full of stumbling blocks. That's because love is a part of life, and life has its ups and downs. But don't worry too much about stumbling blocks. If you stumble, take a moment, get your balance back, and continue on. Now, falling down dead blocks are a different thing. Those you got to worry about.

Lesson 105, Matchmaking Advice from Your Grandma Zelda

Spencer was over six feet tall, built like a boxer with dark brown hair and blue, blue eyes. He was dressed in a custom-made suit, as usual, with perfectly polished shoes and a long wool coat. He was always better dressed than me. He had never been to my below-the-belt happy meadow, but we had discussed it, and it was sort of inevitable that he would spend a lot of time there eventually, which both thrilled and terrified me at the same time.

He cleared out everyone from the house who didn't share the Burger last name, but he didn't have to exert much pressure since the men were panicked by the police presence.

FROM FEAR TO ETERNITY

"Scatter! The coppers are here!" one of them shouted.

"The jig's up!" another one yelled.

"Made it, Ma! Top of the world!"

It was like a movie from the twenties. I expected James Cagney to show up at any minute. Half of the men dropped their mining tools before they took off, and the women were fast on their heels. It was quite a reaction to Spencer. Sure, he was the police chief, but it wasn't like he had brought the rest of the police force with him.

It was a little disappointing, since I never got to hear what Cannes's dark history was about. I began to gather the pickaxes and other tools from Grandma's floor.

"What's going on here?" Spencer demanded.

"I'm cleaning up what could be weapons or play props."

I handed him an armful of tools and took the rest outside to the side of the house. Spencer followed me. "Why were dirty men with pickaxes in your house?"

"I think it had something to do with acting or the real, dark history of our town. Why are you here?"

"I heard that there were men with pickaxes in your house. So, I came to save you."

He dropped the tools on the ground and took mine

from me, dropping them next to the others. A wave of attraction hit me, and sexual chemistry sizzled and popped between us. It took my breath away, and I wasn't the only one who wasn't immune. Spencer pushed me against the house and leaned in close. He was strikingly handsome. I had thought that I would have gotten used to his God-looks by now, but I hadn't.

Damn it.

Spencer had eyes that seemed to look right into my soul and read all of my most intimate thoughts. "What are you doing?" I croaked.

"I'm getting things started."

"Here? Now? Next to the weapons?"

"If I wait to kiss you at an appropriate time in an appropriate place, I'll be an old man with blue balls."

"Blue balls," I breathed.

His hips pushed against mine, reminding me of his tool to get things started. "Uh," I said. He had hot sex shooting out of his pores and through his expensive, tailored suit. His breath smelled of Spanish omelet and coffee. And something else. I was scared of the something else, but I was also hungry for it.

His lips lightly grazed my neck, making me squirm with desire. His lips were like flames, setting my skin on fire wherever they touched. My hands circled his waist and pulled him closer. A thought invaded the far recesses of my brain, warning me that I didn't want this. I tried to push it away, but it was persistent, traveling from the inner recesses of my brain right up to my consciousness. Finally, the thought screamed at me right behind my eyes, and I couldn't ignore it any longer.

I pushed Spencer away from me, unsuctioning his hot lips from my neck. "Wait a second," I said.

He smirked his annoying little smirk. "Why? You wanna get naked, first?"

I so wanted to get naked. "Of course I don't want to get naked! Why would I want to get naked with someone who can't make a commitment.?"

"Define commitment."

"You know. The thing."

"The thing?"

"The thing I said by accident and then you didn't say it, but you wanted to say it. Or you didn't want to say it, but you almost said it before the killer burst in at the cabin."

Spencer's smirk disappeared. "Oh. The thing."

"I'm figuring the thing is why I haven't seen you in the past couple of weeks."

To be fair, I didn't really want to see him, either. The thing scared me.

"I've been really busy, Pinky," he said, using his normal nickname for me. I must have shot him a "that's bullshit" expression because he became sheepish and ran his hand through his perfectly cut hair. "I might have been hiding. But that was before. I'm a new man."

"How much of a new man?"

In answer, he pushed into me and put his hand on the wall above my head. His face was all smolder and hot, hot, hot.

"That's not a new man," I said. "That's the old Spencer."

He arched an eyebrow and shrugged. "It was worth a shot. You want to go to lunch? I'm hearing good things about a new Greek restaurant on Main."

"Like a date? A real date?" I was almost giddy with the idea of going on a real date with Spencer. It was so normal, like it was the start of something real between us.

"What's in a word?" he said like the player he had always been. But I would take it. A date. A date with Spencer. I was officially in a relationship. I finally had a real boyfriend.

"Dolly, you can't go on a date," my grandmother interrupted, popping her head around the corner of the house.

"But…"

She tapped her wrist. "Look at the time. You got to get out of here. John Wayne is only available until noon."

"John Wayne?" Spencer asked.

My heart pounded in my chest, as I remembered that I was being sued. "I'm being sued," I breathed.

"So?" Spencer asked.

"What do you mean, 'so?'"

"I mean, this can't be the first time."

"Of course it's the first time. What did you think? Did you think I get sued every day?"

Spencer shrugged his shoulders. "Well…"

I punched him in the arm. "I got to go. I have an appointment with the second biggest shark in Cannes." I hoped the town's number two shark would save me, and I hoped he would accept a payment plan to pay his bill. Like a three-hundred-year long payment plan.

"At least let me drive you," Spencer said. The month before, a meth lab explosion had killed my ancient Oldsmobile Cutlass Supreme. Now I was carless.

"Thank you," I said, accepting his offer.

Spencer's phone rang, and he answered it. "Yeah. Yeah. Okay. Right." He turned off the phone and slipped it into his jacket pocket. "Sorry, Pinky. You're on your own. I got business."

He stepped away from me but stopped. Turning around slowly, his annoying smirk grew wide into a real smile. He snapped his fingers, like he was remembering something, and walked back to me. He pushed me back up against the house again and moved in quickly, capturing my mouth with his.

The kiss was deep and slow. Full of passion. Heat filled me from top to bottom and a whole lot in between. He pushed his leg between mine and wrapped his arms around me, pulling me close. We were PG-13, but heading into R territory pretty quickly. I knew that my grandmother was watching, but I couldn't stop. Nothing would stop me from kissing Spencer. Nothing. Not wild horses. Not the army. Not a really big stop sign. Nothing.

Then, Spencer stopped.

"See ya later, Pinky," he said with his annoying smirk planted on his face. I stumbled backward a step before I caught my balance.

"What?" I asked, my voice breathy like Marilyn Monroe, but with a heady dose of sexual frustration.

"Talk to you later," he said, walking away from me, his

hand above his head in a backward wave. He walked around my grandmother and out of sight.

Grandma fanned herself. "I need some ice water," she said. "You want some ice water?"

After a glass of water, still in a cloud of Spencer-kissed-me, I dressed in my coat and knit hat. Grandma handed me a scrap of paper with John Wayne's name and address written on it.

"After you see him, stop by Bird's," Grandma told me, self-consciously touching her gray roots.

"Is she okay?"

"She's too focused on her tuchus."

That could have meant a lot of things, and I didn't want to know about any of them. I walked outside into the bitter cold and pulled my collar tight.

A block later, I took a good look at the address on the scrap of paper and realized that the lawyer's office wasn't within walking distance. Once again, I found myself mourning the loss of my Oldsmobile.

To top it off, a glacial gust hit me, and it began to snow.

I dug in my pockets for my gloves, but I must have left them at home. Fabulous. Luckily the bus stop was only a couple blocks away. By the time I got there, my nose was running, and I was freezing. I squinted against the snow to read the sign with the bus schedule on it. *Suck my weenie* was painted across the sign, so I couldn't make out when the next bus was supposed to arrive. I stomped my feet in place, trying to keep warm for ten minutes, but there was no sign of a bus.

Just as I was about to walk back to Grandma's and take my chances of getting sued without legal representation, there was a sound of screeching brakes. A semi-truck stopped in front of me at the bus stop. Its passenger door window opened, and a golden retriever stuck its head out.

"It ain't comin'," a man yelled, sticking his head out the window next to the dog.

"What?"

"Len had emergency gallbladder surgery. No bus today."

"He did?" Who ever heard of a town with only one bus driver? "Are you sure?" I asked.

"Yep. He doubled over at bingo last night and upchucked on the mayor. He was mighty upset since he was two numbers away from winning a new set of chip clips. It's okay, though, since he's planning a side business of selling his

Vicodin pills to his passengers. He might make enough to build a sunroom on his house or an above-ground pool. Oops. I might not have supposed to be telling anyone that. You won't tell anybody, right? Hey, where're you going? I can drop you off," he said, pleasantly.

I told him about John Wayne, and he knew the address.

I climbed into the truck next to him and the dog. Inside was a sea of Burger Boy wrappers and empty Mountain Dew bottles.

And a rifle.

It might not have been wise to let a trucker pick me up, but it was cold, I was late, and this was Cannes, which besides a slew of murders lately, was just about the safest town in America. The trucker closed my window and tossed the rifle in the back

"Going to see the number two shark in town?" he asked, putting the truck into gear and starting off down the street.

"You know him?" I asked.

"Know *of* him. I hear he gets mighty pesky if you say anything about the thing on his face."

"I was warned about his face," I said, making a mental note not to say a word about whatever was on his face. I needed him to like me and protect me from debtors' prison.

The dog licked me and wagged its tail in the trucker's face, making him swerve. "Get in back, Spot," the trucker growled, pushing him out of the way. The golden retriever licked me one last time and jumped to the back. There, it hopped around, still excited for the extra company, or maybe it was always excited to ride in a semi.

Something about the dog's behavior made me nervous, but I couldn't figure out why.

"Colder than my ex-wife before pay day," the trucker noted.

"It's a cold one," I agreed.

He put the wipers on to move aside the snow as it fell. "It's nice to have some company. Usually it's just Spot and me. To tell you the truth, it's a pretty boring job."

"Really?" It was one of the few vocations that I had never tried.

"Occasionally, you run into a sex trafficking ring, and that puts some vinegar in your step, but otherwise, it's a lot of ho hum."

I scooted away from him and clutched the door handle. "Ho hum, huh?"

"Not that I'm involved in trafficking. Don't worry about that. But it's something you see, like pissing on telephone poles."

"Sure. Sure. Like pissing on telephone poles."

The dog paced the back going from window to window, but with the cold weather, there was no way the trucker was going to open one. The dog got me nervous, again, but I didn't know why.

Then it came to me.

I remembered about the gun in the back right before the shot rang out. The dog had jumped once more, this time landing right on the trucker's rifle. The sound was ear-splitting, a huge explosion, when the bullet tore through the front seat, grazed the trucker's shoulder, crashed through the windshield, and sped out into the world, thankfully not hitting anybody else.

"Holy shitballs! What the hell!" I shouted.

The trucker shouted, too, but it was something unintelligible, like *ah-argh-gurgle-blah-oh*. With the shock of getting shot, his foot hit the gas pedal, hard. We were going about forty down Main Street in the small Historic District, which was a fifteen-miles-per-hour zone. I watched in horror as we whizzed by Cannes townspeople in our eighteen-wheeler. It was just a matter of time before we killed someone and / or plowed into Jan's Specialty Foods or the Scrap Metal Coop at the end of the street.

"Slow down!" I shouted.

"I've been shot!"

"Slow down!"

"I've been shot!"

"Brake! Brake! Move your leg!" I urged. Since he was hysterical, I tried to move him and get control of the truck. Unfortunately, his Burger Boy habit had made him too heavy to budge. Not that I could drive a truck, of course, even though I had had a job washing trucks for three hours in Deadwood, South Dakota. I grabbed the steering wheel anyway, and avoided mowing down two moms with their strollers, a golden retriever, and the taco truck.

It was like a video game, but losing would be deadly.

"Oh my God!" the trucker shouted, but I didn't know if he was shouting about the hole in his shoulder or our imminent crash. The end of the street was coming fast, and if we didn't turn, we were going to eat it in the worst way.

The dog barked. The trucker screamed. Yes, my eyes were closed. In recent months, I had had several near-death experiences, and I had found that denial helped a lot in these kinds of instances. So, while we headed toward disaster where the best-case scenario would have us flipping and crashing on the truck's side, I closed my eyes and thought that I should have eaten a third Danish at breakfast.

Luckily, the trucker didn't believe in denial. His survival instinct seemed to kick in when I slapped him hard and screamed at him once again to brake. He finally slammed his foot on the brake pedal. With a harrowing metal-on-metal screech, followed by a smell of noxious smoke, I turned the truck as sharply as I could. We did a ninety-degree turn and, miracles of miracles, like the parting of the Red Sea and Botox, the truck came to a stop.

The semi tilted precariously, knocking gently into Cannes's oldest tree at the side of the road. We were balancing on the wheels on the right side with the left ones up in the air. Gravity was making me slip, but the trucker and I held on, clutching firmly to the steering wheel, as the truck teetered, deciding whether to crash on its side or not.

It didn't look good.

"This doesn't look good!" the trucker yelled.

Just as I thought we were going over, the truck stopped teetering and went the other way, falling back onto the ground with a bounce. Amazingly, all eighteen wheels were securely on the ground. We were saved. The trucker turned the motor off.

"We're alive," I said, completely surprised, checking myself for damage. Somehow, there wasn't a scratch on me. My purse was still intact, too. I checked my eyebrows. Yep, still there. "Are you okay?" I asked the trucker.

elise sax

"I've been shot, you moron!"

I fumbled for my purse to get my cellphone and call 911, but by the time I dug my phone out, we were surrounded by half of the town, and the sound of sirens filled the air. "One firetruck, an ambulance, and three police cars," I muttered. "No. Four police cars." I had a lot of experience with emergency services since I moved to Cannes eight months ago to help my grandmother with her matchmaking business.

The driver's side door creaked open. "You all right in there?" a firefighter asked.

"I've been shot!" the trucker yelled.

"It's not my fault. The dog shot him," I said.

The firefighter peeked his head in. "Hey there, Underwear Girl. Keeping busy?" he asked me. I waved back at him. I had gotten the Underwear Girl nickname a few months back when Cannes's firemen and policemen saw my pink underpants, with me in them.

"I've been shot!" the trucker yelled again, trying to get his attention.

"We're on it, buddy," the firefighter said, winking at him. The firefighter scanned my body. "Looking good, Underwear Girl. I hear you broke up with the tall neighbor of yours."

I nodded. Wow, did everyone in town know my personal life?

"It's not my fault," I repeated. "The dog shot him."

The passenger door opened, and I got a whiff of a familiar men's cologne. I sprouted goosebumps up my legs like a directional sign to my below-the-belt happy meadow.

"Are you kidding me?" he said.

CHAPTER 3

Jerks! We don't do business with jerks, dolly. The world is split between mensches and shmucks—good people and jerks-- and most people are a little bit of both. We can handle those. But the total jerks—you'll know them when you meet them—we don't work with. Tell the jerks where to go. You know what I mean. Tell them to go online. Let Match.com deal with them.

Lesson 103, Matchmaking Advice from Your
Grandma Zelda

It was Spencer Bolton. Again. He always seemed to be there to witness when I wreaked havoc.

"It wasn't my fault," I said.

"I was shot, you know," the trucker reminded everyone. Another fireman helped remove the trucker and give him the care he needed. Meanwhile, Spencer helped me out, and the dog jumped out, too. It stood next to me as if I was its new master.

Spencer looked down at me and smirked his annoying smirk. "You shot a trucker?"

"No, of course I didn't," I said, putting my hands on my hips.

"So, he shot himself?"

"No," I said and bit my lower lip. I glanced at the dog. I knew that Spencer would never let me live it down for being there when a dog shot its owner. I had a reputation for a lot of weird shit. This was way up there on the list. "Is it really important who shot him?"

"Well, yes. Hey, Jim," Spencer called another police

officer. "Is it important to know who shot the trucker?"

"Uh, yes?"

"See?" Spencer said to me. "Jim graduated at the bottom of his class at the academy, but even he knows that it's important to know who shot the trucker."

I looked at my nails. "The dog shot him," I mumbled.

"What did you say?"

I adjusted my purse strap on my shoulder. "The dog shot him." We both looked down at the golden retriever, who wagged its tail and looked up at me, like I was God with a pork chop.

"What did you say?" Spencer repeated.

I turned around and walked away from the truck. The dog followed me. Tea Time was about a half a block away, and I could go for a cup of coffee after my crash. Ahead of me, the trucker was being put into an ambulance, and there was a group of about thirty people milling about. Ruth Fletcher, the octogenarian owner of Tea Time was one of them, and she wagged her finger at me.

"Wreaking havoc with another vehicle," she said. "Two months ago, she ran her car through my shop," she announced to the other people. They all nodded, remembering.

"I wasn't driving, Ruth," I said, pissed off. "And it wasn't my car. It was Lucy's car."

Ruth waved at me, as if I was full of shit. "Semantics."

"No, not semantics. I didn't do anything then, and I didn't do anything now."

"Yeah, the dog shot him," Spencer said. I turned around to him. His lips were plastered together, as he held back laughter. "The dog shot him!" He blurted out louder, like he was reporting on a scene from a Mel Brooks movie. The laughter built up in him. It was obvious that it was stronger than he was and he was about to blow. His face turned red, and he spun around with the effort to maintain some semblance of professionalism. A couple seconds later, it was too much for him, and he exploded, generally becoming hysterical. He roared with laughter and even slapped his thigh. His eyes watered, and his face turned red.

"So sad," Ruth said. "Look what you did to him, Gladie. You're contagious."

The group began to scatter away from the almost-accident, the hysterical chief of police, and the psycho killer golden retriever.

Spencer gulped laughs, trying to get himself together. "The dog shot him," he said, again, shaking his head and putting his arm around my shoulder.

"He did," I whined.

"You're getting better," he said, wiping his eyes. "At least this time, he survived. No dead body for once."

I had run into a large number of dead bodies since I moved to Cannes, and I was getting a reputation for it. "Of course there wasn't a dead body. The shooting was an accident. No murder or attempted murder." I explained to him exactly what happened, and for some reason—probably because of his experience with me or because the trucker confirmed it—he believed me.

Spencer looked down at the dog, again. "Should I read him his rights?" he asked and started laughing again.

I peeled his arm off me and kept walking.

"Spot!" the trucker yelled from inside the ambulance. The dog's ears perked up. It looked at me and then at the ambulance, as if it were choosing.

"I've never had a dog," I told Spencer. I had worked at the Boise animal shelter for six days, but that was it.

"Dog, if you know what's good for you, you'll run like hell," Spencer told the dog. It seemed to listen to him and ran toward the ambulance.

"It must be a male dog," I commented. "I'm not sure I like your advice. Run like hell. What kind of advice is that? I

elise sax

guess if it works for you…"

"Ouch. Pinky, you wound me. I'm not running. But how about we give my cardio fitness a test?" He said the last bit soft and low, speaking in to my ear and making my eyes roll back in my head. "Maybe now we could go to lunch, or even better, we could skip lunch together."

His breath hit my ear with each syllable, and it drove me mad with desire. It was all I could do not to jump on him and give the whole town a live porno performance. But he had reminded me why I didn't have time for lunch. I was being sued. I had to get to John Wayne's pronto and not look at his face.

"I can't. I have to go see the lawyer, but I could go for a coffee first."

We walked toward Tea Time. A sudden wave of relief washed over me. I started looking on the bright side. It was a miracle that nobody else was hurt and that there wasn't more damage. "You know, I kind of saved the town," I said, pleased with myself. It was true. Normally, things blew up and people died, but this time I literally saved the town. "I calmed the trucker down and got him to brake in time. Do you think I'll get a medal or something?"

"Yeah, right."

"I'm serious. I saved the town. I saved the town. I'm like

Superman or Mother Teresa or something."

"Yes. Mother Teresa was known for her truck driving prowess."

I pointed at Spencer, excited. "And she got some kind of medal, right? Or a yacht?"

"The yacht of Calcutta. Sure, why not?"

"So, I'll get something, right?" I really needed something. Money to pay a lawyer. A car. Any body part professionally waxed.

Spencer nodded. "A parade is forthcoming."

"You think?"

"No."

I turned around and pointed at the truck. "Look at that. Can you imagine the damage that would have happened if I hadn't been there? That's a big truck. It could have done a lot of damage." For the first time in hours, I felt like everything would be okay, like no matter how much karmic crap the universe threw at me, I would be able to handle it. After all, I saved the whole town.

"Uh oh," Spencer said, turning me toward him. We locked eyes, and I got the normal, I'm having a seizure, I've got yellow fever, help I'm drowning reaction to the surge of hormones that I got every time I was near Spencer Bolton. I would have bet dollars to doughnuts that he was getting the same reaction. His eyes had turn big and dark, and heat bounced off him.

"Yowza," I breathed.

"You've got that look," he croaked.

"I do?"

"Like you're going to cause trouble."

"I saved the town."

"You saved the town," he said, but he wasn't really speaking. Instead, he was seducing me; his killer testosterone had gone airborne like a virus meeting my airborne estrogen, which had also gone airborne in a desperate need to mingle with his viral testosterone. And boom! Our viral hormones mixed in the middle between us like the world's hottest virtual porno movie.

"Viruses," I breathed.

He stepped toward me, and his arms slipped around my back. His lips were close, closer, closer…Spencer was the world's best kisser. I licked my lips to prepare. Even though we were in the middle of the street, near half of the townspeople and all of the emergency services, I was ready to get this thing between us started. Who cared if I was getting sued? Who cared if I wanted a cup of coffee? We had too many near misses, and it was time to get the show on the road.

Come on, lips. Don't fail me now.

Just as our lips lightly touched, a terrible noise filled the air, making me jump. It sounded like the end was nigh. "What the hell?" Spencer said, standing back out of the reach of my lips.

"Earthquake?" I guessed. The earth did shake, and the noise sounded like the devil himself was climbing up from hell, ripping apart our little town in two.

"Holy shitballs!" I heard Ruth yell behind me.

"Mother of God, the murder girl killed our tree!" another townsfolk yelled.

I assumed I was the murder girl.

"I'm not the murder girl," I yelled back.

"You're kind of the murder girl," Spencer said.

"The tree's fine," I started. "I just winged it. It…"

But Cannes's oldest tree wasn't fine. It had lived through probably one thousand years of snow storms, wildfires, and Cannes's All You Can Drink Night of Mojitos in 2004. It was rumored that Lewis and Clark sat under the tree to eat lunch, and that Bob Dylan wrote "Blowin' in the Wind" about the tree's leaves on one windy autumn day. The tree had survived all of that, lived through all that history, and now it was falling in slow motion, its roots pulling out from the ground.

The oldest tree was beloved by our town as if it was the town's most respected citizen. The tree had stood guard over Cannes since its inception, and now a truck was going to kill it in one fell swoop. All vestiges of hope drained from my body. If I was going to be responsible for knocking over the oldest tree, the town wouldn't let me live for another day. Last month, I was the target of an angry, radical animal rights group, and I didn't want to go that route with tree supporters. I wanted to fly under the radar for a while. Besides, I heard that tree huggers were even more ruthless than animal rights supporters.

"Don't fall. Don't fall. Don't fall," I whispered and crossed my fingers, hoping against hope. But the tree fell, and with it went my medal and yacht. The tree didn't just fall. It fell spectacularly. It crashed onto the truck, smashing it like a Coke can. People ran like cockroaches in a kitchen when the light is turned on. Luckily, the truck was the only victim of the fallen tree.

Except for the tree, of course. It was dead, dead, dead. It was broken into pieces, and branches flew everywhere, like projectiles all over Main Street.

After the noise, the town turned unnaturally quiet.

Shock. I recognized it.

After the running, it seemed like the foot-traffic went in the opposite direction with every person in a five-mile radius coming to see what all of the ruckus was about. When they got a load of what happened, the blame was tossed out my way pretty quickly.

"She did it again," I heard mixed with a lot of "murder girl."

"I have an appointment," I told Spencer.

"Good timing."

"Would you drive me?"

"Where to?"

"A lawyer's office. Someone's suing me, remember?"

"Only one?"

The ride to the lawyer's office was filled with awkward silence. Spencer had left his detective, Remington Cumberbatch—my former casual lover—in charge of the tree aftermath. The fact that Spencer didn't rub it in about the tree and the dog-involved shooting was totally out of the ordinary and proof that he was thinking about us, just like I was.

Us.

Spencer and Gladie.

It was a long time coming, and I still wasn't sure it was smart or had any chance of lasting. We had been avoiding each other, and now here we were in a closed car. Alone.

"So," he said, making me jump in my seat.

"So."

"Why are you getting sued?"

"It's nothing, really." I didn't want Spencer to think that I was a loser. I mean, he already thought I was a loser, but I didn't want him to think that I was an even bigger loser than before.

"So," he said, again.

"So."

"So."

"I don't think we would have been invited to the round table at the Algonquin with this witty repartee," I said.

Spencer took a deep breath. "You like to eat."

I looked down. My coat was covering any bulges that I had acquired during my time with my grandmother. She had a big junk food habit, which I had adopted. "Again, not great with the witty repartee," I said.

"Right. Right," he said, staring straight ahead at the road. "So, tonight I'll be busy, cleaning up the wreck, but tomorrow how about we go to dinner?"

"Oh," I said, surprised. A date with Spencer. It was his second offer of the day. I got giddy, again at the thought of having a "real" relationship with Spencer. "Good. I mean, yes. I like to eat. I mean, I want to go on a diet, but yes, I like food. Ha!" I sort of barked and clamped my mouth closed.

"I rethought the Greek restaurant. There's a new steakhouse a little outside of Cannes. I thought maybe we should start, you know, outside of the town's limits."

"Smart," I said. It would be good not to start whatever we were starting under the microscope of Cannes's residents.

"Seven tomorrow?"

"That sounds good," I said. "But what will I eat between five and seven?"

"Okay. Five." Spencer parked in front of the small house where the lawyer's office was located. "Which will seal us never getting an invite to the Round Table."

I unlocked the door and stepped out, wondering if maybe we were supposed to kiss goodbye. What were the rules to this relationship? I had no idea. At least we were off and running. A real date. And steak would be involved. I couldn't ask for more than that. Well, maybe dessert.

"See ya," I said, awkwardly. Spencer had leaned over, probably to give me a kiss goodbye, but now I was out of range, so I awkwardly waved goodbye and slammed the door shut.

"Smooth, Gladie," I said out loud.

Spencer's car peeled away from the curb. I watched him drive toward the scene of my last disaster. I looked at the house. With all of the excitement, I had pushed the lawsuit to the corners of my mind, but now reality was knocking on my brain again.

The house was a tiny, wooden one-story building, most likely built during the gold rush in the 1800s. Outside, there was a large wooden sign with *John Wayne, Attorney at Law* written in large black letters. I walked up the three steps to the front door and tried to open the door. But the doorknob wouldn't turn. I could hear a voice from the inside, so I knew that someone was inside. Searching around the door, I found a series of buttons under a screen. I pushed one of the buttons.

"Hello?" I said. "I'm here to see John Wayne? I think my grandmother made an appointment?"

I had an urge to turn around and run in the opposite direction. I had never hired a lawyer, and the idea freaked me out. The only experience I had with lawyers was working as the lunch cart girl for six days in a New Jersey law firm. And those lawyers were scary. They were more interested in biting the heads off other lawyers than eating anything on my lunch cart. I was just about to turn around and walk away from Mr. Wayne's office when the monitor came to life, and a woman's face appeared. She was young and scarily thin with big earrings and slicked back hair.

"Yes?" she said with an English accent.

"My name's Gladie Burger. I think my grandmother made an appointment for me with Mr. Wayne."

The woman sneered, and the door beeped. I lunged for the doorknob and opened it. Walking into the house was like stepping into another world. Every inch of it was white, black, glass, and chrome. It was the modern of modern, the classy of classy. John Wayne's office was chipping away at my self-confidence. I didn't do well with fancy.

Suddenly I fought the urge to fart, and I could feel a big booger in my nose.

The sneering woman approached me. She wore a tight miniskirt, braless in a white silk shirt, and four-inch heels with pointy toes. She was a dead ringer for Cruella de Vil.

She looked me up and down in slow motion and didn't look impressed with what she saw. I would have bet my last dollar that she hadn't pooped in at least four years out of sheer will over her colon, as if poop was beneath her. I surreptitiously sniffed my armpit to see if I had remembered to put on deodorant this morning. I didn't smell too bad, even after the crash.

The interior walls were made of glass. That's how I could see a man in his office yelling on the phone, waving his arms wildly. I assumed it was John Wayne, even though he looked nothing like his namesake. First of all, he was half the movie star's size. Almost.

He was wearing a very expensive suit, even nicer than Spencer's. As he spoke, he paced, and when he turned, he spotted me and put his finger up in the air as if he either wanted me to wait for him or he was checking the wind direction.

The English, constipated, anorexic woman looked down her pointy nose at me. "Would you like a water?"

"I guess so?" I said like a question.

She sneered and walked away. "I'll rip your head off and shit down your throat!" Wayne yelled from his office. "Yeah. Yeah. Sure. Let's do lunch next Wednesday. Love to your wife."

He hung up and walked out. "John Wayne, but everyone calls me Duke," he said, extending his hand. Duke was in his fifties, and he would have been a good-looking man except for his face, which had a prominent Hitler mustache. I couldn't draw my eyes away from it.

His face.

His Hitler face.

His little Hitler mustache under his nose, drawing my eyes to it.

I couldn't even blink. It was transfixing. Nazi transfixing. Panzer division, Mein Kampf, bunker transfixing. No wonder I was warned not to mention Duke's face. It was everything I could do to stop myself from mentioning it. My lips quivered with the question demanding to be released from my mouth.

Why?

Why oh why oh why a Hitler mustache?

I mean, why?

There had to be a story there. Who grew a Hitler mustache? I decided to charitably think that his facial hair only grew right under his nose.

I shook his hand. "I'm Gladie," I managed.

He nodded. "The unjustifiably persecuted love broker? Come into my office."

I sat down on a chair in front of his desk. He paced his office. He spoke a mile a minute, sometimes spitting when he got extra excited. "If that moron Zorro thinks he's going to crucify my client, he needs more electroshock."

"Crucify? Electroshock?"

"You know he's been going around saying that I'm second shark in this town? Second shark? And what's that supposed to mean? That he's first shark? Have you heard of such a thing?"

"No," I lied.

He slapped his hands together. "This is the case I've been waiting for. The big drawn out, media whore, publicity tsunami, clusterfuck case of a lifetime. We're going to be front page of the LA Times. We're going to be on The View."

"The View?"

"The View."

I loved Whoopi, but I didn't want to be on The View, and I didn't want a clusterfuck case of a lifetime. I scratched at a mosquito bite on my hand and wondered if it was really necessary to have a Hitler lawyer.

Probably.

"The thing is that I don't have a lot of money."

"Don't worry. I understand your situation. I can do it for one."

"One?" I asked. One thousand was a lot more money than I had in the world, but with a payment plan, I could just about make it. "I think I could do one thousand dollars. Thank you."

His Hitler mustache twitched. "Funny. Not one thousand dollars. One hundred thousand."

"Uh…"

"That's a steal for this kind of case."

"Steal's a good word. But maybe we can settle the case."

"Settle? Settle?" His voice rose and cracked with emotion. "You're up against Gordon Zorro. He doesn't settle. He won't stop until you're flayed alive. Do you know what flaying is, matchmaker lady? Flaying hurts. A lot. You'll be kaput. Destroyed. The only thing standing between you and total devastation is me. I'm Checkpoint Charlie. I'm the thin red line. You need me. I'm your only chance. Otherwise you can kiss away any chance of happiness in your life. Do you want to kiss away your happiness?"

I shook my head and fought back tears. I didn't want to kiss away my happiness. I wanted to be happy. I had just started to do well as a matchmaker, and now I had a real date with Spencer. Even though I didn't have a car and I had killed Cannes's oldest tree, I finally had hope that things were looking up.

"I want to be happy," I said. "But I don't have a hundred grand."

Duke leaned down until his face was only an inch or two from mine. "But you have a house."

"Excuse me?"

"An historic house right in the center of the Historic District, and it's worth a goodly sum."

"I don' t have a house. My grandmother has a house," I said, disturbed. It was one of the original houses, a large Victorian, probably built by one of the newly rich gold miners in the 1800s.

Duke's breath was sour, and his Hitler mustache seemed to announce his bad intentions. "I'm sure your grandmother wants the best for you."

I nodded, not sure where he was going. "You want her to sell her house?"

Duke stepped back and sat on the edge of his desk. "No, nothing like that. She signs it over to me, and I let her live there for the rest of her natural life."

"What?"

"It's a win, win, win situation. Your grandmother helps you and stays in her house. You get your life back. I get a house in a few years. Your grandmother is quite elderly, right?"

A chill went up my spine, which was weird since I was boiling mad. Threatening my livelihood was one thing, but nobody threatened my grandmother. Sure, he was talking about taking her house after she died, but he was talking about her dying and taking her house. I never thought about my grandmother dying, and I certainly never thought of anyone taking her house. My grandmother was her house. Her house was my grandmother. Our family had lived there for over a hundred years, and it was Grandma's identity. Since the day that my father died when I was a child, Grandma never left her property. Her house was her safety blanket.

"Don't look so distraught," he said, smiling. "Between you and me, I have a lot of experience with this. Most people can't afford a good attorney. So, I provide this service. It's painless."

"Painless."

He nodded. "Yes. Believe me, I've got it down to a science. I've done it dozens of times."

I stood up and smoothed my skirt. I was fighting mad on my grandmother's behalf. I adjusted my purse strap on my shoulder. "Listen, Adolph. This is one Poland you're not marching into. So, take your jack boots and retreat. Do you hear me?"

He stood and ran a finger over his mustache. His smile was gone, and his bully lawyer attitude was back. "You don't want me as an enemy, girlie. This offer is on the table for twenty-four hours and not a second more." I walked toward the door. "You'll be begging me for help. Think hard before burning this bridge."

I took a deep breath and stormed out of his office, past the skinny, constipated woman, holding a blue glass bottle of water. "Is that for me?" I asked and grabbed it. At least I would get some free fancy water out of the whole thing.

I left and stood on the lawyer's front porch, trying to catch my breath. My blood pressure was through the roof, and it was no wonder. I didn't have an attorney, and now Zorro was going to flay me alive.

CHAPTER 4

Perception is reality. I heard that on a show once. A very thin lady talked about branding and making enough money to buy a yacht, a big apartment in Manhattan, and a young man named Paolo. All it took to get this branding was to pay the thin lady three hundred dollars, and she would make you a whole new you in people's eyes. I'm not talking about a makeover where you wax your eyebrows and get hair extensions. I mean, a whole new you! I mean, people would say: "Who's that? It looks like Sally, but Sally is a nebbish with a Volkswagen. The new Sally in front of me is a star and deserves a Mercedes SUV. Here, Sally, take my money, and I will give you a Mercedes SUV." Such a deal. Branding. Perception. What a crock of shit, bubeleh. They can kiss my tuchus until Tuesday with that baloney. You are who you are. You're my sweet dolly. Don't try to be anybody else. Besides, you would get seasick on a yacht.

Lesson 38, Matchmaking Advice from Your
Grandma Zelda

My cellphone rang. "Hello, Grandma," I answered.

"Don't forget to visit Bird, bubeleh."

I had forgotten. Bird had missed her weekly appointment with Grandma, and she was worried. Her salon was a long walk from the lawyer's office, but I needed the fresh air.

"Okay."

"I'll have food ready for you when you get home and I won't let the tree huggers in."

Sometimes it was good to have a grandmother with a third eye. I didn't want to explain to her about the tree, so it was a relief that she somehow already knew. I hung up and put the phone back in my purse.

The walk to Bird's salon almost relaxed me. The air was cold and fresh. Cannes looked beautiful in the winter white. I was almost happy to be without a car.

When I finally got to the salon, I realized that something wasn't right. Usually, Bird's salon was a beehive of activity with a steady stream of customers coming in and out. But now it was down to a slow trickle. Inside, it was business as usual except for Bird's chair, which was empty. Bird normally handled three customers at once, dyeing one person's hair while cutting another's, and there was always a large group waiting for their turn.

But not today.

"Hey, Gladie," the manicurist greeted me and handed me a clipboard. "Will you sign?"

"Sure." There were pages of signatures. I signed on line number three-hundred-forty.

"Great. Can you believe about the tree? We're going to get justice." She took back the clipboard and tapped it with her other hand. "This will get us started."

I looked at the clipboard, suspiciously. "Uh, what did I sign?"

"Thank you, Gladie! Gotta get back to the pedicure. Calluses from hell."

"Do you know where Bird is?" I asked, as she walked toward a woman, who was soaking her feet in a large bowl.

"Upstairs. Always upstairs."

Always upstairs? Bird had an apartment over the salon, but she was never there, no matter what the pedicurist said. Bird was more than a hairdresser and a salon owner. She was a woman on a mission. As far as she was concerned, there was nothing more important in the world than beauty maintenance. A woman with roots or large pores or—gasp—one too many hairs on her chin was heresy to Bird's upkeep religion. So, normally Bird was never in her apartment. Instead, she could always be found behind her chair, handling the town's needs in a blur of activity, unless she was doing emergency house-calls to women like my grandmother, who couldn't leave their homes.

I walked to the back of the salon and through a small doorway to a narrow, circular stairway to the second floor. I knocked on Bird's door, but there was no answer. I could hear her from inside, and she didn't sound like herself. Bird was always serious and firm, but I could hear panic in her voice.

I tried the doorknob and was surprised when it turned, and the door opened. "Hello? Bird? You there?"

The apartment was a mess, like it had been ransacked by a home invader. From the other room, Bird screamed.

I grabbed an umbrella from next to the door and wielded it high above my head. "Bird? Bird?"

I found her in her living room in front of her big screen TV. She was standing with a big mask on her face, headphones over her ears, and in her hands, she was holding on to two small batons. She shook them and spun around. "I got you, you bastard!" she shouted.

"Bird! It's me! It's me!"

"I'm Radan the Horrible!" she exclaimed. "And I will burn down your castle and pillage your women!" She spun around again, shaking her hands.

"Well, this is different," I muttered.

I approached her, carefully stepping over dirty laundry and discarded water bottles. I called her name again, but she obviously couldn't hear me. On the television, a complex game was playing. It was some kind of medieval world filled with monsters and aliens. Bird didn't strike me as a gamer, but she was really into it. I tapped her shoulder, and she jumped a mile in the air.

She ripped the headphones and mask off. "What the hell?" she asked, blinking, as if it was hard to focus on the real world. "Gladie? What are you doing here?"

"Grandma sent me to check on you. You missed yesterday's appointment."

"Zelda's appointment isn't until Monday."

"It's Tuesday."

"No, it's not. It's Thursday." She picked up her cellphone and checked the screen. "Oh my God."

"Have you been playing your game since Thursday?" I asked.

Bird smiled, and I got a whiff of her breath. Holy Moses, it smelled like something bad died in her mouth. A really smelly thing. That wasn't the only thing off about her. Her outfit was dirty and wrinkled. She didn't have any make up on, and… "Bird, you have roots. There's gray roots on your head."

She didn't care. Her smile was frozen on her face. "I wonder how much I've lost," she said, dreamily. She trotted to the bathroom, and I followed her.

"Are you okay?"

In the bathroom, she stepped on a scale. "Three more

pounds," she said, still lost in some kind of euphoric dream. She clutched my arms tightly and got in my face, giving me more of her killer breath. "Gladie, you have to try this diet."

"Low carb? I really like bagels."

She swatted the air, like low carb was an irritating fly. "Not low carb. Virtual reality gaming. It stops you from eating. I'm never hungry. Never. When I'm in the mask and headphones, I don't care if I ever eat again."

"Sounds good," I said. I knew the look of a cult follower when I saw one. I had had a lot of experience in that arena. And the one thing I knew about an over-stimulated extremist was to back away slowly. I wasn't going to convert her. Her Silicon Valley habit needed a professional. She needed a diet deprogrammer. Grandma was right about Bird. She cared too much about her tuchus. Although to tell the truth, her tuchus looked pretty damned good. She was on her way to a size double-zero. She was so skinny that soon she could have her own television show playing the wife of a fat, old comedian.

Bird walked back to the living room and put her mask on. She didn't even pee first. Ignoring me, she put her headphones on and shook her baton-laden hands, whirring the game back into action.

"Okay, I'm out of here," I said. I felt guilty abandoning Bird in her time of need, but I knew I needed to call out the big guns for this particular emergency. Grandma would know what to do about Bird's new diet.

Outside, I took a deep, healing breath of cold air. I wanted to go home, eat some lunch, and take a nap. I deserved it.

Suddenly, the weather took a bad turn. A frigid wind whipped my face, and I turned up my collar. Another gust hit me, and it began to snow. It wasn't the usual dry, powdery snow that Cannes enticed Southern Californians with to visit the town in winter. No, this was wet and icy. The wet cold seeped into my bones, and I shivered. I was already miserable. I longed for my Cutlass Supreme with its working heater, but my beloved car was in Oldsmobile heaven.

That's why it was weird to see my Cutlass Supreme driving toward me. I stumbled backward in surprise. I had to be hallucinating, I told myself. My longing for my beloved car had caused a crazy, realistic hallucination. I was seeing things. I was tripping like Bird, maybe caught up into her virtual reality where exploded, incinerated cars came back to life and drove down the street as if they were totally fine. I touched my face to make sure I wasn't wearing Bird's mask. No. I was really there, out in reality reality instead of virtual reality, cold and getting wet on the sidewalk on Main Street.

But my car was still driving toward me. Maybe I really died in the truck accident, and I had joined my car in heaven. Or maybe I was still alive, but my car was possessed like I was living in a Stephen King novel. How did that book end? Did the car owner survive?

As the car got closer, I noticed that it was in better shape than my car, which had had more rust than paint, dents pretty much everywhere, and a trunk that was tied down with rope. The Cutlass Supreme driving toward me didn't have a scratch on it. It looked brand new, even though it was an old model like mine.

I slapped my forehead. Of course, it wasn't a Stephen King car. It wasn't possessed. No, it was Ruth Fletcher's car. She rarely took it out since she worked at her tea shop all the time. Ruth was an ornery old lady and gave me a hard time more often than not, but there was a good chance she would give me a ride since the snow had turned to sleet, and I had a long walk ahead of me.

I jumped into the street and waved my arms, wildly. "Stop, Ruth! Stop!" I called out. Her car braked, swerving. I ran toward it and opened the passenger door. Before I sat down, I did a quick search to make sure there weren't any firearms. Nope. I should have known, because Ruth hated the Second Amendment more than she hated coffee drinkers, and she really hated coffee drinkers.

I got in and closed the door behind me. "Thank you, Ruth. Oh, it's toasty in here. Nice."

"I only stopped because I didn't want your dead body

parts to mess up my car," she growled.

"I appreciate it. Can you take me home?"

Ruth rubbed her chin. "I don't know. You're kind of bad luck to vehicles…and trees."

"I'll be on my best behavior."

"That'll be a first. Okay. Sure, but I'll take you on an errand with me first. It'll be better to have you there as a buffer."

I probably didn't want to be a buffer, but I was thrilled to be out of the cold. "Where are we going?"

Ruth grumbled low in her throat, as if we were heading to a proctologist appointment or an Adam Sandler movie. "I have to visit my older sisters."

"Your *older* sisters?" I asked. Ruth was old. Really old. I was pretty sure that she had been at Pearl Harbor and the Trojan War, but I wasn't positive. She threw me the evil eye with my age comment. "I didn't know that you had any sisters," I said, covering my tracks.

"I don't see them much. Old people give me the creeps."

"Me, too."

"All that thin, crepey skin and bad breath. And why

they don't put in their damned hearing aids is beyond me. Every hour I spend with them is full of 'Huh? Huh?' It's enough to turn me into an axe murderer."

I was reasonably sure it wouldn't take much to turn Ruth into an axe murderer. "When you say 'older,' how much older are we talking about?"

"One day Methuselah visited them, and he said, 'whoa, those are some old dames.'"

I didn't know who Methuselah was, but I figured that they must be really old. "So, like one hundred? Two hundred?"

"Two hundred? What's the matter with you?"

"Well, you said they were older."

"I said, older, not immortal. They're both ninety-three. Twins. Naomi and Sarah. Be careful of them. They're not as nice as I am."

We drove the rest of the way in silence. It was nice to be back in an old Cutlass Supreme. I missed mine something awful. It was as big as a boat and a real smooth ride. We drove out of the Historic District and up further into the mountains to the outskirts of Cannes itself.

The landscape was snowy white and beautiful. I could see deer running between the trees on the side of the road. With the radio off, it was dead silent, except for the sound of the sleet hitting the car as we drove.

"This is nice," I commented.

"It used to be," she said. The wild countryside changed suddenly as we turned onto a wide, paved road. We passed a sign with *Apple Serenity Village* written on it.

"Hey, I know where we are," I said. Apple Serenity Village was a newish retirement community for old people with big bucks. If they were at least sixty-five years old with a seven-hundred-seventy-five credit rating and a boatload of cash, they could buy a luxury, handicapped-accessible home within an easy golf cart distance from a community center, mini-mart, and a passel of on-call healthcare workers, who made house-calls. I couldn't wait to get old and live in Apple Serenity Village. It was crazy nice. As far as I could tell, there were four house models, each pretty similar to each other, which repeated over and over to form a neighborhood of thousands of houses. They were all immaculate with clear walkways and driveways, as if it was someone's job to clear the snow as it fell.

"How much do you think these houses go for?" I asked.

"Seven hundred for the three bedrooms. Six-twenty-five for the two bedrooms."

I sucked air between my teeth in shock. "Are you kidding me? That's insane. What are the walls made of? Gold? Hey, wait a minute. How do you know the prices? Are you thinking of moving in?"

"Are you kidding? I'd rather do the nasty with Kissinger than live with these retired capitalists and rapists of the earth."

"Sorry. Sorry," I said, putting my hands up in surrender. I guessed that Ruth's sisters were more than happy to live with retired capitalists and rapists of the earth, though, and that rubbed Ruth the wrong way. Hence the need for a buffer.

Ruth turned onto a small road, which was different than the rest of the development. It was covered with gravel, and it dead ended a short distance away with a grand manor. There was no other way to describe it. Surrounded by overgrown trees and bushes, the house looked to be around the same age as my grandmother's house, but this one was twice as big with turrets and balconies, alcoves, and sunrooms.

"Holy cow. Is this where your sisters live, Ruth?"

She parked in the driveway and turned off the motor. She took a deep breath, and I noticed that her hands shook slightly. "You okay? You want me to call a doctor?"

"Only if it's Doctor Kevorkian," she muttered and opened her door. I got out. I needed to pee, real bad. I hoped they had running water.

We walked up the porch steps. "This house looks so different from the rest of the retirement village," I said.

"It's the original house. We sold the rest of the land to the corporation who built the development."

I stopped in my tracks. "'We' sold? 'We' sold? You must be loaded, Ruth."

"It wasn't my idea to sell. I was outvoted."

"You must have millions. Millions. More than one million. Lots," I breathed thinking about what it must feel like to have millions. I would have bet that it felt better than only having eighteen dollars and a pending lawsuit against her.

Millions. Wow.

Ruth turned toward me. She was wearing a turtleneck and men's slacks under a long wool coat. The skin of her face hung down a few inches from where it should have been. Her hair was thick and entirely gray, cut just below her ears. She wagged a long, bony finger at me. "Keep that under your hat, Gladie. I mean it. Don't spread it around. It's nobody's business. I don't want it getting around."

"What's it worth to you?"

Now, normally I was a nice person. I helped people when I could. I even recycled bottles. But Ruth had given me a hard time since I moved into town, deriding me for every drop of coffee I drank. She deserved to be given a hard time, even if it wasn't outright blackmail. It would kill her communist self for people to know that she was a millionaire, one of the chosen few, the one-percent, the corporate greedies. So, I sort of had her over a barrel.

"I do like your lattes," I said, rubbing my chin.

Ruth stared at me, like daggers were going to shoot out of her eyeballs. I took a step back just in case. Maybe baiting her wasn't a good idea, after all.

"One free latte per week," she offered. Her lips were pursed in a tight straight line, like she had fought against letting the words out of her mouth.

"Millions. I bet they'd put you on the board of the Chamber of Commerce. Maybe you'll get a statue in Reagan's library. That's not too far from here, right?" It was fighting dirty, hitting her below the belt. She was such a liberal that when she drove, she only knew how to turn left. Never right.

"Reagan's library?" she screeched, her face completely drained of color. She crossed her arms in front of her. "Fine. Free lattes for a year."

"Free lattes for a year," I breathed, hopping on my heels. Santa Claus really did exist. Never again would have I have to scrounge for dollars to get my caffeine fix. Never again would I have to worry that my credit card wouldn't go through for the two-fifty latte. Sure, I was technically committing a felony, blackmailing her. But coffee is coffee. "Thank you, Ruth. Thank you." I pumped her hand in appreciation, even though she didn't seem happy about the deal we struck. The door opened, and an ancient face appeared.

"Ruth? Is that you?" she asked, looking right at me.

Ruth pushed past me and into the house. "Of course that's not Ruth. Put your damned glasses on, Naomi."

"Huh?"

"And put your hearing aid in."

I put my hand out, and Naomi shook it. "I don't moisturize enough," I told her. She was dressed in head-to-toe pink in what I thought was a vintage Chanel suit. On her head was a pink pill box hat to match.

"Oh, a visitor. We love visitors." She let me in, and I stopped just inside the door to take it all in. The house was filled with over one hundred years of furniture and knick-knacks. It was a tchotchke explosion. HSN could have done a bang-up business if they got their hands on this place. Every inch of wall was covered in paintings. Every surface was covered in old photos. With Ruth, her sister, and everything they owned, the theme was definitely all about the old.

"Is this your family home?" I asked Ruth's back as she walked away from me through the parlor and down a hallway. She didn't bother to answer me. Except for the smell of mothballs, I found the house pretty calming. There wasn't a lick of technology anywhere. It was like the world had slowed down just for them. It was the complete opposite of Bird's video game diet world.

I liked it.

Ruth's sister Naomi put her glasses on, which had been hanging around her neck on a gold chain. She looked me up and down. "You're not Ruth," she said.

"I'm Gladie. Gladie Burger. I'm Ruth's…" I couldn't exactly say 'friend.' What was I?

"You must be Zelda's granddaughter. I used to babysit her."

"You did?"

"Terrifying little girl. Every month, she would tell me when I would get my period, like she was connected to my uterus or something. Still, she did win me a mint at the track, so I can't fault her for being…you know."

I knew. Most of the town was more than happy to have my grandmother find their soulmates for them, but she did get more than her share of witch comments. Grandma took those in stride, saying it was worth it to have the gift for matchmaking.

"Look! We have company!" another old woman exclaimed, walking into the parlor. She was wearing overalls and a frilly shirt, and she was drying her hands on a kitchen towel.

Her face was streaked with some kind of food substance, and I was pretty sure there was flour in her hair. Otherwise, she was a dead ringer for Naomi. Identical.

"This is my twin. Sarah," Naomi told me.

They had aged the same. Both of their faces had drooped and sagged at the same rate. Each line was identical. Even their neck warbles were the same. "Nice to meet you, Sarah."

"This is Zelda's granddaughter," Naomi explained.

"Are you a witch, too?"

"It skipped a generation," I said.

Ruth stomped back into the parlor, holding a giant wrench, which was dripping something onto the worn oriental rug. "She's not a witch. There's no such thing as witches. When will you two old crones grow up?"

"I have a Ouija board here somewhere," Sarah continued, ignoring her younger sister. "Maybe you could reach Daddy for me? He left me his baseball card collection in his will, but I can't find where he hid them."

"Uh…" I said.

"She's not a witch," Ruth repeated.

"And maybe you could contact my old beau for me,

too?" Naomi asked, clapping her hands together in glee. "I haven't seen him since we went to the VJ dance in '45, but I'm sure he must be dead by now."

Ruth stomped her foot and waved her wrench while she spoke, as if she was using it to enunciate her words. "She's not a witch. She's a matchmaker...sort of. Occasionally she finds dead people, but she doesn't talk to them."

I nodded. "That's true. I don't talk to them."

"Pity." Naomi's head dropped forward, as if she was looking at something on the rug, and her pill box hat slipped a little off her thick, gray bun, dropping a bobby pin to the floor.

"We'll get out of here soon," Ruth said, going back into the kitchen with her dripping wrench.

"I guess I could Ouija a little," I told Sarah. I didn't like to let people down, especially when they probably didn't have long to live. I had never used a Ouija board, but I understood how it worked. I didn't believe that there was anything supernatural about it, and I figured there was more than one heavy finger that had pushed the piece around, giving the players the message they were looking for.

"Hear that, Naomi? She's going to talk to Daddy for us. This is wonderful. You know, sometimes I think I like the company of the passed on more than the company of those who are still with us."

I didn't know how to respond to that, so I just nodded and took a seat in one of the old-fashioned arm chairs. I sat back against the handmade afghan that was draped over the chair. Naomi went off to search for the Ouija board, and the doorbell rang.

"I'll get it," Sarah said, adjusting the straps on her overalls. She opened the door, and an old man walked in. "Oh, Mr. Foyle, how are you? You're looking well."

"What? What?" he said, like he was a World War One-era British general. He looked like one, too. He was bald with bushy eyebrows and a thick mustache that was growing over his lips into his mouth. He wore a long overcoat, which was coated in a layer of snow. "Colder than a whore's ass in bankruptcy court," he announced, signaling to Sarah to help him remove his coat. She put it on a brass hook by the door. He straightened his suit jacket, which was pin-striped and made to measure. He wore shiny black shoes, and a purple pocket square.

"Would you like some tea? We were just about to contact Daddy."

"I wouldn't mind some tea, if you got something to put in it." He walked a few steps into the parlor and stared at me with unblinking eyes.

"Mr. Foyle likes to sit in that chair when he visits, Gladie. You wouldn't mind, would you?"

"Of course not," I said, standing. Mr. Foyle side-stepped around me and plopped down on the chair. He unbuttoned his jacket and got comfortable.

"This is Gladie Burger, Zelda Burger's granddaughter," Sarah said. "Gladie, this is Dwight Foyle, retired."

"Zelda Burger? Is she a resident?" he asked.

"No. She lives off in the Historic District, not in Serenity Village," Sarah explained.

"I found it," Naomi announced, walking down the stairs with a box in her hands. "It was in the attic, wedged between Grandmother's newspaper collection and Uncle Fredrick's toy horse. It's pretty beat up, but I think it'll still work. Oh, hello there, Mr. Foyle," she said, seeing him for the first time. "Do you want to talk to your late wife?"

"What? What? My late wife never had anything to say when she was alive. I doubt she got more interesting after being dead for twenty years. Sarah, didn't you say something about bourbon?"

"Oh, the tea," she said, clapping her hands together and doing a little jump. "I forgot. I'll get it immediately."

"Make mine chamomile," Naomi called after her, placing the Ouija board box on the coffee table. "I don't want to get too excited. You know, in case we really do reach my old beau."

She knelt by the coffee table, and her knees cracked. Her pillbox hat slumped to the side, and she took it off, removing a long, sharp hat pin. She placed it inside the hat next to the Ouija board and opened the box. It was a normal Ouija game, but extremely old with an all-wood planchette piece, instead of plastic. Naomi took it out, and a dead spider plopped down on the board.

I stepped back in case there were some live bugs in there.

"Now, I'm pretty sure it's rare to open a portal to hell with a Ouija," Naomi said, happily. "It almost never happens. So, we don't have to worry about demons coming out and possessing us."

"That's a comfort," Mr. Foyle said.

Naomi giggled. "Although it might be fun to spin my head around a little. And talk in tongues. Oh, wouldn't that be fun?"

I was pretty sure that wouldn't be fun. "You know, Naomi, Ruth was right. I don't think I'd be good at this game."

She swatted the air. "Oh, pshaw. I'm sure you'll be great."

Sarah returned, rolling a cart with a large tea service on it. "I brought some homemade sour cream cake to go with it," she announced.

"Daddy's favorite," Naomi said. "Very thoughtful. He'll love some when he shows up."

Sarah served the tea, and I took a slice of cake. She poured a shot of bourbon into Mr. Foyle's tea. Ruth's sisters and I sat on the floor around the coffee table. I took a bite of the cake and washed it down with some tea.

"Oh for the love of Hubert Humphrey," Ruth complained, walking into the parlor, holding the same dripping wrench. "I told you she isn't a witch."

"Sit down and have a cup of tea," Sarah said.

Ruth perked up. "Tea?" She sat in an armchair next to Mr. Foyle and took a cup of tea. "Who are you?" she demanded.

"What? What? I'm Dwight Foyle, retired."

"I don't believe in retirement. I never give up. Never," Ruth said, sipping her tea. "Who the hell invented retirement? It's like an advertisement to the universe that you're ready to curl up and die. Is that what you want to do? Curl up and die?"

While everyone waited for Mr. Foyle to say if he wanted to curl up and die, I took another slice of sour cream cake. I hadn't eaten lunch yet, and I was starving. The sugar was also helping me stay calm with the threat of demons and hell portals in front of me.

"I'm not going to curl up and die," Mr. Foyle said, understandably affronted. "Between you and me, I've got a story brewing."

"What do you mean, a story?" Ruth asked. "Are you a writer?"

"Mr. Foyle used to be a reporter in Los Angeles," Naomi said. "He did a big exposé on soup lines."

"Soup lines, huh?" Ruth said.

"Shall we?" Sarah asked, placing the planchette on the middle of the board. She put her fingers on the edge, and Naomi followed. They shot me a look, waiting. I couldn't help but worry that this was one of those life-changing moments, a before the portal to hell was opened moment. I didn't want to open a portal to hell.

"So, what kind of story is brewing?" Ruth asked Mr. Foyle, making me jump.

"Big one. Big one. Going to blow the roof off this part of the country. Front page story. It might get me killed."

"How so?" Ruth asked. "Are the fascists after you?"

His eyebrows knit together, making it look like he had a fur scarf on his forehead. "What? What? Fascists? No. No. But I have some powerful people upset with me."

"Gladie, let's start," Sarah urged. "I'd like to get my hands on those baseball cards."

I'm terrible with peer pressure, even when my peers are seventy years older than I am. "Okay. Here we go," I said and put my fingers on the planchette piece.

"Daddy? Are you there?" Naomi asked the ceiling.

Nothing. No *woo-woo* or shadowy figure or movement on the board. And no open portal to hell, thank goodness.

"Father isn't there," Ruth said. "His body turned to dust forty years ago in the Cannes cemetery."

Then, the piece moved. It moved fast around the board, spelling out *Shut up, Ruth.* And then *Cards are in the coffin with me.* And finally a message that no one understood: *Be careful what you drink.*

Then, the Ouija board went dead, like our money ran out on a payphone call.

"That's it?" Naomi asked the board. "No word from my beau?"

"What does that mean, 'Be careful what you drink'?"

I took my fingers off the board and surreptitiously looked under the coffee table to check for demons. Nope. Nothing. Not even a dust bunny.

"How did I get born into this family?" Ruth complained and drained the last of her tea.

"What are you looking for, Gladie?" Sarah asked.

I sat up straight. "Nothing."

"It's a shame about the baseball cards."

"Come on," Ruth grumbled. "One of you pushed the piece around." She looked at me pointedly when she said "one of you," and even though I didn't push the piece around the board, I blushed.

"It was Daddy," Naomi insisted and began to pack the game back into the box.

I took a breath, relieved. Maybe Ruth was right and one of her sisters had pushed the piece around. No dead person talked to us. No demons. No portal to hell opened. I took another slice of cake and popped a piece into my mouth. Yum. It was more delicious, now that the specter of specters was out of the picture.

"I ain't afraid of no ghosts," I mumbled.

Like an answer from the underworld, there was a chilling whistling and banging coming from the kitchen. "Daddy?" Sarah asked.

"It's not Father," Ruth grumbled. "It's the damned pipe

that I haven't finished fixing." She put her tea cup down on the coffee table, grabbed her wrench, and stood. "Give me some help, Gladie."

I had no idea how to fix a pipe. Plumbing was one of the few temp jobs that I never had. But I wanted to put space between me and the Ouija board. Besides, my legs were falling asleep, sitting on the floor, and Ruth's sisters were talking to Mr. Foyle about his prostate. Time to go.

"Let's make this fast," Ruth told me when we walked into the kitchen. "This place gives me the heebie jeebies. Old people coming and going all the time."

"Kind of like Tea Time."

Ruth rounded on me, pointed her wrench at my face. "This place is nothing like my tea shop. Nothing. Apple Serenity Village is filled with ultra, self-entitled corporate goons and their widows. My tea shop is patronized by worthy people with good taste who are prepared to pay for quality. I mean, except for you."

"If I didn't know better, Ruth, I would say that you are fond of your customers. But that can't be right."

Ruth's eyes squinted into narrow slits, but she lowered her wrench. "I hate rich people."

"But you're rich."

"I'm not rich. I have money. There's a difference."

She began to rant, and for the first time since I moved back to Cannes, I was in the clear of her ranting. I wasn't in her crosshairs because one thing was sure: I wasn't rich. Ruth ranted for a good five minutes about the rich invaders of her childhood home until she was interrupted by an angry pipe under the sink that had had enough and decided to explode.

"Charge!" she shouted and went after the pipe. She drafted me as her assistant, and by the time she fixed it, I was soaked through.

"Is it done? Is it fixed?" I asked.

"Yep." She mopped up the floor and closed the cabinet under the sink. "All done."

"How come you're clean and dry, and I look like I just did three laps at the community pool with my clothes on?"

"Do you really need to ask?"

I dabbed at my wet shirt with a kitchen towel. "I'm going to freeze my ass off outside like this." A mosquito bite was making me crazy, and I scratched it. "Pneumonia and covered with mosquito bites. I'm so unlucky."

"Let's get Sarah and Naomi to give you a change of clothes. And that's not a mosquito bite," Ruth said.

She left the kitchen, and I followed her.

"A change of clothes? What kind of clothes?"

"Clothes, Gladie. Dry clothes. Beggars can't be choosers."

She had a point.

The parlor was empty. No sign of Ruth's sisters or Mr. Foyle. "Where the hell did they go?" Ruth demanded.

I scratched another bite on my arm.

"Does Zelda know about those bites?" Ruth asked.

"Of course she does. She's got them, too. Mosquitoes have invaded her house.

Ruth scowled at me, like it was preschool and I had eaten the supply of paste. "It's not mosquitoes. Those are bed bug bites."

"They're what?"

Ruth looked around the empty room. "I bet they went up to take naps. I think there are some blankets in the window seat. That'll do until I get you home."

She pointed at the window seat by the beautiful picture window. The seat was covered with an embroidered cushion. As far as I was concerned, blankets were better than Depression-era

FROM FEAR TO ETERNITY

hand me downs. I walked toward the window to get the blankets.

"When you say, 'bed bugs,' do you mean a kind of mosquito? Like a mosquito indigenous to Cannes?" I asked Ruth.

"When I say 'bed bugs,' I mean the small blood-suckers that live in your mattress and come out at night to eat you alive while you're asleep. Your house is probably infested."

Something inside me told me that Ruth was right, but I decided that the something inside me was a liar. "Infested is a big word," I said, opening the window seat. "Let's not jump to conclusions. Let's adopt a positive attitude."

"I'm positive that you've got bed bugs. How's that?"

I turned away from Ruth. Sometimes her ornery attitude was too much to handle, and I just wanted to grab a blanket and head on home. I opened the seat cover all the way and looked inside.

"Oh!" I gasped and fell backward onto the floor, letting the window seat slam shut.

"What's wrong?"

"It's Mr. Foyle," I said, staring at the window seat.

"What about Mr. Foyle?" Ruth demanded, impatient

with me.

"He took your advice."

"What advice?"

"He curled up and died."

"What the hell are you talking about?"

She stomped over to the window seat and opened it wide. "Holy FDR and the Public Works Administration," she breathed.

I stood and peeked inside the seat, again. Poor Mr. Foyle was curled up inside, his bushy eyebrows brushed up against his thighs. He didn't move. Not a breath.

"Amazing how he fits in there," I said. "It's like a carnival trick. You think he climbed in to see if he could fit and then dropped dead?"

"You think he's dead?" Ruth asked.

"Oh, yes. I mean, I don't often see them intact like this, but I know dead when I see it."

CHAPTER 5

"There you go, again." Ronald Reagan said that. It was fine for him, but you don't ever say that to a match. There are those, through no fault of their own, who just do the same thing over and over and never seem to progress. But one day they will. It's your job to keep them upbeat and pat their backs when they're down. Believe that they will graduate from "there you go, again" to "there, you did it."

Lesson 71, Matchmaking Advice from Your
Grandma Zelda

I had never seen Ruth scared before, but there was no doubt she was scared now. Or it could have been a big case of being flustered tinged with anger. Or gas.

"Weird how you were just talking about him curling up dying, and then here he is," I said, staring at the dead man. He wasn't exactly peaceful because death wasn't peaceful. But he had no obvious signs of trauma. No blood. No bugged-out eyes. No bruises.

He was just dead.

"Are you saying I cursed him?" Ruth demanded.

"No," I said, but I wasn't sure. Was it possible to curse someone? Everyone accused my grandmother of being a witch, but maybe Ruth was the witch. "Of course you didn't curse him," I assured her. "Did you?"

"Why the hell is he in the window seat?" she asked, ignoring my question.

"It's like he's hiding."

Ruth closed the window seat quietly. "You're not going to tell anyone about this," she told me. We were nose to nose. She was older than dirt but full of life. Scary, aggressive, meaner than spit life.

"But he's dead, Ruth. We have to tell someone. You're probably in shock." Awkwardly, I patted her back. She knocked my hand off of her.

"I'm not in shock. I'm thinking clearly. You can't tell anyone about this."

"But…"

Ruth slapped the side of my head, and I yelped in pain, clutching my head.

"Think about it, girl. There's a dead man hidden in my

sisters' window seat," she growled.

"I know. I have eyes, Ruth. I saw him plain as day. Dead in your sisters' window seat. Oh…." It came to me like a lightning bolt. "You don't think your sisters hid him in the window seat, do you?"

"No, I think you were right, and he got in the seat to see if he could fit and dropped dead."

"You do?"

"No!"

"But why would your sisters do that?"

I waited for an answer, but Ruth's mouth wasn't moving. Instead, she stepped closer, and her eyes darted back and forth, as if she was trying to communicate something to me with her eyeballs. It worked.

"Noooooo," I said. "You don't think that your sisters…"

"Listen Gladie, my sisters voted for Nixon. Twice. You know what that means?"

Damn. I hated history. "Give me a minute," I said, trying to remember my tenth-grade American history class.

"It means they're mean, Gladie. Really mean. Enemies list mean, Gladie."

I looked at the embroidered window seat cover. "Kill the neighbor mean?"

"It's a possibility."

I clutched onto her arms. "Kill the neighbor and stuff him in the window seat mean?" I looked around for Ruth's sisters. I had a sudden need to get the hell out of there.

"Do we have a deal? You're not going to say anything?"

"Well…" Deal? Deal? The second I got to safety, I was going to call the police department and alert them to the dead guy in the window seat. I was going to shoot fireworks, carry neon signs, whatever it took to tell the authorities that there was a dead journalist stuffed into a window seat.

I tried to hide my plans from Ruth, making my face into an inscrutable expression of ambiguity. It didn't work. I wasn't much for inscrutability or ambiguity.

Ruth narrowed her eyes and scowled at me. "Gladie, you're already called the 'death girl.' Do you want to have that nickname forever?"

A couple weeks before, I had found dead body parts in a box store. I figured my nickname was stuck on me like white on rice. But Ruth's desperation to protect her sisters was tugging at my heartstrings. Not to mention I didn't want to lose my deal for free lattes for a year. Could I really just forget about a dead man stuffed into Ruth's sisters' furniture?

No. No, I couldn't.

"Ruth, you're not thinking clearly. There's a dead man in the window seat. Dead. He's not breathing. We can't keep this secret. He's going to start to smell. And people are probably waiting on him. He's nearly late for the early bird special or whatever old people eat."

Ruth crossed her arms in front of her and scowled more severely.

"Suspicions will grow when he doesn't cash his social security check," I continued. "People will guess something's up when JCPenney's stock of patent leather shoes doesn't move. Ditto nose hair shavers. Think about it, Ruth. We can't keep this secret." My voice rose at the end, and I tried to calm myself down. "Listen, I'm sure your sisters have a perfectly good explanation about the dead journalist in their parlor. I'm sure it's some kind of misunderstanding. Maybe some kind of sex game gone wrong. I hear a lot about old people and sex games now that Cialis is covered on Medicare B. Yeah, it's probably that. A sex game. Old people getting it on. A threesome, hide-and-seek, contortion kind of sex game. Doesn't that make you feel better?"

"Girl, how do you manage to find two brains cells to rub together so you can talk?"

I didn't know how to respond to that.

"Do we have a deal?" Ruth demanded.

"I'm sure it's going to be fine." I was almost relaxed, a by-product from riding a high-horse. I couldn't remember the last time I was on the calm side of a massive freak-out. It felt great. I patted Ruth on the back. "It's going to be fine," I repeated, but I was interrupted by loud sirens coming our way, and I jumped, clutching onto Ruth.

"They're after us!" I shouted. "They know! They know!"

Ruth pushed me away from her. "Get ahold of yourself, girl. Of course they don't know." She glanced at the window seat. "I'm reasonably sure that they don't know. The sirens are probably not for us. Serenity Village is chock full of strokes and heart attacks. The sirens are probably for them."

In unison, we shuffled to the window by the front door and pulled the curtain to the side. Outside, two cop cars were driving toward us with their lights flashing and sirens blaring.

"What's the prison sentence for hiding a body?" I asked Ruth.

"Play it cool, Gladie. Don't say a word. Not a peep."

"What if Mr. Foyle's family is worried about him?"

"He doesn't have a family."

"How do you know?"

"Shut up. The fuzz is here."

She pointed outside. Spencer and Officer James were walking up the stairs to the front porch. I broke out into a doozy of a flop sweat. I wiped my forehead on my sleeve.

I opened the door just as Spencer's fist was poised to knock on the thick wood. His face registered the moment he recognized me with complete shock. His mouth dropped open, and he was struck speechless.

"I didn't do anything," I blurted out.

"Pinky?" His face was almost boyish, as if he had stumbled on Santa Claus in his living room.

"I didn't do anything."

"Well, that would be a first. What are you doing here? Why are you soaking wet?"

I yanked on Ruth's arm, pushing her in front of me. "Tell him, Ruth."

"Hello, good-lookin'. We were just fixing my sisters' pipes. What do you want? Do you have a search warrant? I'm not letting you in without a search warrant."

Spencer furrowed his brow, like he was trying to figure out if we were hiding a dead man in the window seat. I gasped and choked on my own spit. Ruth threw me a look that could kill.

"Pinky, what have you done?" Spencer asked wisely. I was about to spill the beans when Ruth elbowed me hard in my ribs. "Haven't you wreaked enough damage to this town today?" he continued.

"The other thing wasn't my fault," I said, affronted.

"I've had to spend the entire day handling the disaster you did with the truck."

"I wasn't driving," I whined.

"If I had a nickel for every time you've said that."

"I'll second that," Ruth said.

"I've had to haul away a truck, haul away a gigantic, old tree, clean up the mess, and contend with tree huggers, who are the scariest bunch of folks I've ever dealt with," he said, counting on his fingers. "I don't think I can handle any more of your chaos."

I was fuming with the anger that came from being wrongly accused. It occurred to me that Spencer wouldn't let me hear the end of it if I announced about the dead guy. It also occurred to me that I hadn't eaten lunch.

"Why are you here?" I demanded.

"We got a report that there was a man living with a deer, and we came to extricate the deer."

"What the hell? Are you making that up?"

"I'm the Chief of Police of Cannes. I don't make anything up."

"He's here to save a deer," I told Ruth, thankful that he wasn't looking for Mr. Foyle.

"I know who you're talking about," Ruth told Spencer. "He's two doors up. Freak with a deer."

"Freak with a deer," Spencer repeated.

"See? I have nothing to do with it," I said, victorious.

Spencer took a step backward and stopped. "We're still on for tomorrow evening, right?" he asked, sheepishly.

"Sure, but don't say another word about chaos or blaming me for anything."

"Deal," he said, and I shut the door, throwing my back against it. I tried to catch my breath.

"Nosy bastard," Ruth grumbled. "Jack-booted, fascist, police state, knocking on doors in the middle of the night, terrifying innocent people."

"Give it a rest, Vladimir," I said. "You've got twenty-four hours. Then, you're going to report it and keep me out of it. You understand?"

Ruth didn't look happy about it, but she nodded. "Fine. Twenty-four hours, and I'll tell him. Keep you out of it."

elise sax

"Good thinking about the man with the deer. Got rid of Spencer quickly."

"I didn't make that up. This town has gone to hell in a handbasket."

Since I was hungry for a real lunch away from dead bodies, I let her comment lie there. I didn't want to know any more about the town going to hell, but I had a sneaking suspicion she was right. Even more than that, I worried that Ruth and I were going to hell. Poor Mr. Foyle, dead in the window seat. And what about Ruth's sisters? There had been no sign of them since we fixed the pipe in the kitchen.

I put my coat on over my wet clothes, and we walked outside to Ruth's car. "You're going to handle this, right?" I asked her.

"This ain't my first rodeo," she said, not bothering to be more specific than that.

I sat inside her car, and she started the motor. A man in boxer shorts and snow boots ran in front us, illuminated by Ruth's headlights. He was running fast, perhaps to keep up with a large deer, which was tethered to his waist with a pink leash.

"You may be right about the hell thing," I said.

"You think you've seen everything, and then a man in his underpants runs by with his companion deer. Sometimes I wish I would have been a smoker so I'd be dead by now."

FROM FEAR TO ETERNITY

She put the car into reverse, and we caught an eyeful of Spencer and Officer James as they ran after the man and the deer. "Stop! Stop!" Spencer yelled. It wasn't his finest moment.

"You know, the cop's got great stamina," Ruth noted, backing out of the driveway. "That might come in handy for you."

We drove to Grandma's house in silence. I could sense the heavy weight of responsibility on Ruth's shoulders. Even if she wasn't that fond of her Nixon-voting sisters, she didn't want them to be murderers. I didn't know what she could change in twenty-four hours. Maybe she just needed that time to come to grips with the situation. Suddenly, I was happy that I left Mr. Foyle to rot, curled up in the window seat.

Sort of happy.

Ruth drove through the Historic District on our way to Grandma's. Even though it was bitter cold and still snowing, the sidewalks were filled with people, more than a few dressed as trees and others in 19th century garb, who had seemed to set up sides about the founder's play. Artistic differences. The worst kind of difference. But Founders Day play actors aside, I had a bad feeling about the trees. They looked like they were out for revenge. I hoped they didn't have my name and address.

"I've got five-hundred-dollars on Jose's team to win," Ruth said.

"I'm still confused about what they're fighting about."

"The whole stale annual founders play they put on. Some say

97

they got the history wrong, and others don't care if it's wrong. The old guard doesn't want to change the play. I think they should just make the damned changes, show this town for what it really is. You see, some people don't like change. But I like change."

I exploded into laughter. "You like change? *You* like change?"

"Calm yourself, Joan Rivers. I like change. I'm a progressive. Anyway, I think Jose is going to win. This town was founded by racist bastards, and he knows it. Besides, he has access to power root grinders. The other side doesn't have a chance."

She turned into my grandmother's driveway. "Don't say a word," she warned as I opened the door.

"Twenty-four hours," I warned back.

It felt great to have something over Ruth for a change, even though it was a horrible thing to hold over her. She scolded me on a daily basis, and now I was the responsible one, and she was the one who wanted to leave a dead guy in her family home's antique furniture. Ruth was right. It was nice to change.

So, I walked up the rest of the driveway to my grandmother's house with a new feeling of maturity. I opened the door and walked in. The house was packed, as usual. Putting my coat in the closet in the entranceway, I searched for my grandmother. I was starving, and it was now past lunch.

"Leftovers in the kitchen," Grandma called from the parlor.

"Chili cheese dogs."

Chili cheese dogs. Yum. Perfect for the weather. My stomach growled, thinking about them. I had a tinge of diet guilt because I had adopted my grandmother's junk food habit since I had moved in with her, but seeing Bird's complete breakdown in an effort to be eternally skinny made me toss away any diet guilt I had, at least for the moment.

As I passed the parlor, I peeked in. There was a group of about ten women, sitting in a circle. They didn't look familiar, but it wasn't uncommon for people to come from out of town to get a dose of Grandma's services.

"In twenty-five years, my husband couldn't find my clitoris," one woman complained, bitterly. "He had me believing that I didn't have one. He said, 'Rachel, some women just don't have one.'"

"Oh, it's gaslighting," another woman erupted.

"Gaslighting!" Rachel agreed. "Finally, I realized that he wasn't trying that hard to find my clitoris. Hell, he probably didn't try at all!"

The women applauded her epiphany. My grandmother opened the hutch behind her and pulled out a small box, which she handed to Rachel. "Here you go," she told her. "It's a vibrator. Top of the line. You might not find a man who will find your clitoris, but *you'll* know exactly where it is."

I couldn't figure out if it was some kind of new age class or what, but I made a mental note that Grandma had stashed sex toys in the hutch. That nugget of information could come in handy if the whole Spencer thing was delayed any longer.

In the kitchen, four chili cheese dogs were waiting for me in a pile on the table. "Four?" I said to the empty kitchen. "I can't possibly eat four." I hoped I was telling the truth, but I was reasonably sure I was lying.

But it was true that I was starving. I hadn't eaten lunch, except for the sour cream cake. I opened the fridge and took out a can of root beer. I sat down and took a bite of a chili cheese dog. I wondered when Grandma's class would be over because we had a lot to talk about. She needed to be updated about John Wayne, Bird's habit, and the possibility that the house invader she worried about was really a swarm of bed bugs.

"Hello, Underwear Girl," a muffled voice said. I turned around in my chair to see Fred, the local police department's desk sergeant and my first match. He was wearing a large mask, as if he was starring in a disaster movie about a virus gone bad. He was also wearing a brown uniform with a *Kill the Critters* name tag. He held a sprayer attached to a large, metal canister.

"Whatcha up to, Fred?"

"Protecting your house from creepy crawlies," he said and sprayed the counter to prove his point. A cloud of poisonous gas floated above the counter and over the table. I breathed in a bunch of it and hacked it out of my lungs.

"I don't think you're supposed to be doing that," I said after I caught my breath.

"It's my job now, Underwear Girl. It's what I do."

"What are you talking about? You're a police officer."

Fred peeled the mask off his face and let it rest on his head. He wiped his nose with the back of his gloved hand. "That's before I became a criminal."

Last month, Fred discovered that his landlady was a meth drug lord. "Now, I'm an exterminator," Fred explained. He didn't sound very happy about it. "I thought it would be a lateral move. I still get to kill things and protect and serve."

"I don't think you should feel guilty about what happened. The whole town was fooled."

"You don't understand, Underwear Girl. I'm a trained peace officer. I should've known. Now I gotta do what I gotta do. At least I can save you. Your grandmother says you got a whole heap of bed bugs in the house."

He shuddered, and his face drained of all color. "You okay?" I asked and helped him to a chair. I gave him a glass of water, and he gulped it down.

"Don't tell anyone, but I'm not a big fan of bugs," he said, softly.

"Then I guess you're in the right business. Killing them, I mean."

That seemed to perk him up, and he smiled. "You sure look pretty today. Are you dressed up for something special?"

I looked down. I was still soaked through, and I had been so excited to eat that I had forgotten to change. Now, my lunch was coated in toxic chemicals. "Actually, I was just about to change," I told Fred. "Are you done spraying?"

"I haven't started. I need to look at the bedrooms."

"Follow me. I'll show them to you."

We walked upstairs. Fred held onto his sprayer, like he was brandishing a weapon, expecting zombies to attack him at every turn.

"I haven't seen any bugs at all," I assured him, as we got to the second floor. "Did my grandmother say she had seen some?"

"No, she called and said that Ruth had told you that you had bed bugs."

"She did?" It was like having the NSA monitoring my every move. If only my grandmother could tell me who killed poor Dwight Foyle, but she was always quick to say that her third eye didn't see murder.

"Here we go," I said, walking into my bedroom.

"What a pretty room, just like you," he gushed.

"Thanks, Fred."

"I'm supposed to look under the mattress," he said and blanched, again.

"Maybe you can go back to police work, Fred. It would be much calmer on your nerves."

"No, this is my fate. The justice system doesn't want a criminal like me."

"Strictly speaking, you're not a criminal."

He shook his head, determined to punish himself. "No. I have to do my time." He slipped his mask back on and took a deep breath. "Here I go."

Like a dead man walking, he went to the bed, lifted the head of the mattress and looked underneath.

Even through his mask, his scream was shrill and deafening. In a panic, he jumped back and began to spray all over. He sprayed the ceiling, the walls, the floor, and me, but missed the bed, entirely.

"There's millions of them!" he shouted and ran out of the bedroom. I ran after him. He kept spraying and screaming all the way down the stairs.

Once he reached the first floor, he spun around in a circle, spraying in an hysterical attempt at eradicating every bug on the planet before they could spread their cooties to him. That was unfortunate for Grandma's group, which had come out to see what all the screaming was about and got dosed with the spray for their efforts.

Fred took off again, this time headed back to the kitchen.

"It's just Fred. He's killing bed bugs," Grandma explained, appearing from the parlor. She was the only one who hadn't been sprayed in the house. Her and the bed bugs, that is.

There were a lot of murmurs about bed bugs from Grandma's matches, and then the women quickly made excuses about why they had to leave early, all the while dusting off their clothes with their hands. Within seconds, they were gone, and it was just Grandma, me, and Fred's screams in the house.

"Poor Fred," Grandma said.

"I hope he doesn't have a heart attack."

The screams got louder and were followed with a few loud noises, like the kitchen was being destroyed. I ran into the kitchen and found Fred frantically slapping at the back door's doorknob. He had thrown his mask off and had tossed his spray can onto the counter, breaking the coffee maker and a panini press. He finally managed to turn the doorknob through his gloves and opened the door.

"Uh," I said, as he ran out into the backyard. I ran out onto the back stoop, and Grandma came out, too.

Fred was standing in the middle of the backyard, still screaming. His eyes were closed, and he stomped around in a circle in the snow, all the while ripping his clothes off.

When he was down to his boxer shorts and work boots, Fred stopped screaming and with one last shudder, stood peacefully in a state of shock, like he didn't know how he ended up half-naked in Zelda Burger's backyard in the middle of winter.

"I'm seeing a lot of boxer shorts today," I told my grandmother.

"I'm a tighty-whitey woman, myself."

"Fred, what are you doing?" I called.

He blinked. "Underwear Girl?"

"Bring him in, bubeleh. Give him a chili cheese dog," Grandma instructed.

"The chili cheese dogs were exterminated."

"There are pizza bagels in the freezer."

I picked up Fred's clothes, handed them to him, and we walked back inside. He got dressed in the kitchen, while I nuked the pizza bagels. We shared them, but Grandma wasn't hungry.

"So, Fred," I started when we were into our second pizza bagels.

"About my bed."

"The horror," he moaned.

"Bed bugs?"

"We're going to need a bigger boat," he moaned, again and shuddered.

"You've seen worse, though, right?"

"I see dead people."

"But you can fix it, right?"

"Come with me if you want to live!"

"I think he's gone, Grandma," I said. "He's on a movie loop. He might need electroshock."

My grandmother put her hand on Fred's arm. "Fred, dear, you're safe, now. Safe."

Fred blinked. "Safe?"

"Yes. You saved us all."

"It was a close one," he said. "They had me surrounded. I thought I was a goner, for sure. I wish I had my gun."

I was never so thankful that Fred didn't have his gun.

"You were very brave," Grandma told him.

FROM FEAR TO ETERNITY

Fred blushed and swiped at the air in an *aw, shucks* gesture. "Just part of the job, Mrs. Burger."

"Tell me what the damage is," Grandma urged him, gently. "Are you going to have to spray?"

"I'm going to have to look at my field manual, but I'm pretty sure we're going to have to tent with this kind of infestation. Three days."

Grandma and I exchanged a look. If the house was going to be tented for three days, where would we go? I could stay with a friend, but my grandmother hadn't left her house since I was a child. When she was sick, she got house-calls. Now, a little tiny bug was going to kick her out and I didn't know how she was going to deal with it.

"Don't worry about it, dolly," Grandma said. "Fred can set up a tent outside for me to stay in."

Fred nodded. "I can do that. I got a good one from when I was a Scouts leader. Don't worry. It won't be pumped with poisonous gas like the tent over the house. I got an air mattress, too, if you want. It'll be good when the bugs are all dead."

I couldn't imagine my grandmother camping in the backyard in the middle of winter, sleeping on an air mattress.

"I got a contact over at Cannes Cable," my grandmother explained to me. "He can rig the tent so I won't miss out on my programs."

elise sax

She seemed totally unconcerned. I was sure that she had it all figured out, so I didn't point out that it was freezing and there was a growing layer of snow in the backyard. I knew there was no point arguing with her about staying. She knew plenty of friendly people in town who would be happy to put her up for a few nights, but my grandmother refused to leave her property line, even when her house was pumped full of poison.

Fred gave us a lecture, reading from his technician's manual on everything we needed to do to prepare for the bed bug removal. It was a daunting task, including washing all of our clothes and linens. Every time he mentioned the bed bugs, he would get pale, and he looked like he was going to pass out. Poor Fred. He was so upset about our bed bugs that I had forgotten to get upset about them, myself. Not to mention, I was being sued, the tree huggers were angry, and there was a dead man rotting in Ruth's sisters' house. Bed bugs came a distant third in my list of things to worry about in my life.

Once Fred was completely recovered, he left to make plans for our tent. Meanwhile, Grandma got on the phone and started making calls for assistance in setting up her backyard accommodations. I prepared the house to get poisoned. It was a long afternoon of getting organized. Finally, I ordered Chinese food, and we sat down at the table in the kitchen again to eat in peace and quiet.

"It didn't work out well with John Wayne?" Grandma asked.

I'd almost forgotten about the lawsuit. I had no lawyer and no options. I was going to wind up as a secondary character in a Dickens book, and those characters didn't end up well. What was I going to do? Would I have to go to debtor prison?

"I got a bad stink off him, Grandma. He's not a nice person."

"I guess you'll have to go about it a different way then. Go to the source."

"The source?" I had no idea what she meant by going to the source.

Grandma nodded. "What happened with Bird?"

"Bird is in a really bad state."

"I was afraid of that. She's gotten carried away this time."

"I'm afraid that she needs some kind of deep deprogramming or major intervention. It's like she's sitting next to Jim Jones, about to drink the Kool-Aid. Or about to take a nap with Heaven's Gate. It'll probably take a while to get her free. Maybe we can get somebody else to come and do your hair."

We threw away the Chinese food cartons, and Grandma turned off the kitchen light. "I couldn't do that to Bird," she said, as we walked upstairs to bed. "I'll just have to wear a turban and closed toed shoes for a while." It was a sacrifice for her. Grandma liked to look her best. "It's going to take some thinking about what to do for her, though. I don't see her coming out of this on her own. We're going to have to help her."

I didn't know what she meant by "we." How were we going to help her? Did "we" include me or somebody else? I hoped it didn't include me. I had enough on my plate without having to take away Bird's video game diet. Bird was a lot stronger than I was, and I didn't think she would take too kindly to me taking away her virtual-reality.

Upstairs, I called my best friend Bridget and asked if she could house me for the next three nights.

"That would be great," she said. "Perfect timing since tomorrow is prenatal yoga. You didn't forget, did you?"

Bridget was pregnant and bound and determined to turn her unborn baby into a super human, which wouldn't have been so bad if she wasn't also determined to drag me along with her in her quest. Prenatal yoga, prenatal educational classes, prenatal consciousness training. She had drafted me to go with her to about a dozen different wacko mommy classes.

But I wasn't a mommy, and I wasn't sure I ever wanted to be a mommy. I was pretty sure I didn't want to have a super-human fetus, though. Bridget wouldn't admit it, but I realized that she dragged me along because there was no father in the picture. For sure, I didn't want to be a father, but best friends were best friends, and I wouldn't abandon her in what was probably the most important time of her life.

"I wouldn't miss it for the world," I said.

"Good. I'll see you tomorrow. I can't wait to tell you about the person I found who can make male fetuses get in touch with their feminine side."

"Sounds good," I said even though I had no idea what she was talking about. Bridget was a strident feminist and liked to protest pretty much everything. The idea of bringing a male child into the world had her completely freaked out, even though she was doing her best to make sure that her son would be a card-carrying member of NOW.

After our call, I brushed my teeth and slipped on sweatpants and a man's T-shirt along with athletic socks that Spencer had left in the house a few months before. I was exhausted. What a day. I wondered what normal people did to fill their days. I doubted it included watching a dog shoot a trucker and finding a dead man in a window seat.

But that was just a guess. I didn't have a lot of experience with normal people.

The moment my head hit the pillow, my fatigue washed away and was replaced by a surge of adrenalin brought on by a good dose of fear. What had Fred found under my mattress? I debated with myself whether I should look, but I came down firmly on the side of *no way*. Fred had told me that bed bugs came out when they sensed a person was sleeping, and now I was determined to stay awake so that they wouldn't eat me alive.

I laid that way for a long time, battling between my exhaustion and my paranoia, which wasn't actually paranoia because there really were bed bugs out to get me.

Finally, I rolled off the bed, taking my blanket and pillow with me. There on the floor, my exhaustion took over, and I fell into a deep sleep. This time, there was no dream about Spencer and his gorgeous body. This time I dreamed that bed bugs were swarming all over my body, eating me alive. It wasn't as good as a Spencer dream.

In the middle of my nightmare, I was woken up suddenly. A strong hand shook me awake and then clamped down hard on my mouth so I couldn't scream.

"Don't scream. Don't talk," the raspy voice instructed me in the dark. "I need you to come with me."

CHAPTER 6

Expect the unexpected, bubeleh. It sounds easy enough, right? It's all about making plans. Make a plan for every eventuality, and you'll be fine. Right? Wrong! What a pile of drek! It's like the calendar in those fakakta phones. It takes fifteen minutes to push all the buttons to make a note about your haircut appointment, but then you remember your appointment is at the same time as the season finale of Supernatural, and then it takes another fifteen minutes to change the haircut appointment. You could die from such planning! Listen, dolly, your matches can push buttons all day and night, clutching onto their fakakta phones, like they're five years old and Apple made the perfect blanky. But they're just wasting time. They might as well stare into space and pick their noses because it'll do about the same to control their futures as all the plan-making in the universe. Tell your matches to be up for anything and not get discouraged if things don't go like they expected. In other words, shit happens. Go with the flow.

Lesson 23, Matchmaking Advice from Your
Grandma Zelda

I was terrified. Woken from a deep sleep with a hand on my mouth in the dark, I was sure I was done for. Then, I smelled the familiar scent of Shalimar, Earl Grey, and righteous indignation, and I knew I was going to be okay. "Ruth? Is that you?" I asked, pushing her hand off of me.

"Who else would it be?" she demanded. It could've been anybody. Tree huggers, an angry match, or at least a dozen other suspects.

I sat up. Ruth was kneeling on the floor next to me. "What are you doing here?"

"I need you to come with me."

"Why? What did I do?"

"Nothing, for once. I need your help."

I rubbed my eyes. "What? You need my help? I must be dreaming. Did I do a Marilyn and take a couple Advil PMs too many? You need my help? What?"

"Don't give me lip, girl. Don't make me say it again. I don't beg. Get your ass up and come with me."

"What's the matter?"

"Believe it or not, I can't sleep when I know there's a dead man in my sisters' house." She flipped my cheek hard. "Sorry," she said. "Bed bug. It was biting your face."

I jumped up and shook my clothes. "Oh, my God. It's like a horror movie. I'm being eaten alive in my sleep. They probably gave me cholera or the plague or something. My God, Ruth. I probably have cholera."

"Do you even know what cholera is?"

"Or maybe Ebola," I moaned.

"Hurry and help me up. I'm kneeling on eighty-year-old knees. Do you think that's easy? I haven't had cartilage anywhere in my body in twenty years. My bones are halfway to dust. What the hell were you doing on the floor, I have no idea. Made me kneel on the floor. What kind of selfish girl are you? Only thinking of yourself. Come on, let's get going before Zelda wakes up."

Ruth let me take the time to slip a pair of boots on but drew the line at letting me get changed or peeing. We tip-toed downstairs, and I got my coat out of the coat closet. Outside it was bitter cold and completely quiet.

"What time is it?" I whispered.

"A little after two. Come on."

I opened her car's passenger door and looked up. The sky was awash in bright stars. I could even see the Milky Way. It was breathtaking. I had never seen so many stars. It made me believe in magic, in the smallness of humanity and the grandeur of nature.

"Get your ass in the car," Ruth hissed. "Did you get lobotomized or something?"

elise sax

I got in and closed the door. "Ruth, you are always sweetness and light."

"It's a burden," she said and backed out of the driveway.

The entire town was sleeping. There wasn't a sign of life anywhere. We drove through the Historic District, and Ruth turned left where the truck had taken down the town's oldest tree. There was a large memorial in its place. Piles of flowers lay on top of the snowy sidewalk, and there was a neon sign flashing *Tree Hater Beware* in red and green.

I swallowed.

"You sure like to stick your foot in it," Ruth commented.

"It wasn't my fault. The dog shot the trucker."

"Huh," Ruth grunted, like that said it all.

I wished my life ran smoothly. Living in a small, bucolic village, in a beautiful Victorian house, working to help people find love should have been a guarantee for a quiet, stress-free life. It should have been a lock. But since I had moved in with my grandmother, it had been nonstop chaos and trauma. It was only a month since I had been hunted by a radical animal rights group. Now, tree huggers were angry at me. It was like I was enemy number one against nature.

Like a thunderbolt there in the front seat of Ruth's

Oldsmobile, I decided once and for all to change my life. From now on, I was going to lead a normal, stress-free life. I had the foundation for it, including the start of a real relationship with Spencer. It was a done deal, I decided. I was only a hop, skip, and jump away from enlightenment.

"Buddha," I said out loud.

"What?" Ruth asked, driving out of Cannes in the direction of her sisters' house.

"So, you never told me how you want me to help you." I had blindly followed Ruth out into the night just because she asked me. Of course, it had something to do with the dead guy in the window seat. But what?

"I'm hiring you."

I gasped and choked on my spit. I coughed and sputtered, trying to get air. "You what?"

The car swerved, and Ruth got it back on track. It started to snow, and she turned on the windshield wipers. "I want to hire you, okay? Do we have to dwell on it?"

"You want to hire me as a matchmaker?" She was old, but I was taught by my grandmother that love wasn't bound by age. Not to mention that Ruth had a boyfriend who she dug up any time she had a social engagement.

"Of course I don't want to hire you as a matchmaker.

elise sax

Do you think I'm crazy? I'm hiring you to investigate the death of the man in the window seat."

"You're hiring me? Like I'm Sherlock Holmes?"

"Believe me, if I could get Sherlock Holmes, I wouldn't be hiring you."

"Like Jessica Fletcher? Like Miss Marple?" Then it hit me that Ruth wanted me to investigate a murder. It was crazy timing since I had recently decided to dedicate myself completely to being a professional matchmaker, and not two minutes ago, I had decided to lead a normal, unexciting life.

"I'm not a professional detective, Ruth. You should call the cops."

"No way. I hate my sisters, but I'm not serving them up to a corrupt, Gestapo, corporate-bought, sieg heil, sadistic police department."

"I'm not sure they're sieg heil. They sponsor an annual Girl Scouts cookie sale."

"Don't get me started on the Girl Scouts."

We turned onto the Serenity Village's property. "Okay. Okay. But how do you know I can help? I'm a matchmaker, not a detective. Besides, I don't want to help. I have a career to get going, a life to live. And I'm not sure it's legal to keep this secret."

"Just until you solve the mystery. That shouldn't take you too long."

"Are you kidding? Listen, I don't solve mysteries."

Ruth parked in her sisters' driveway and turned off the motor. She turned toward me. "Bullshit," she said.

"Bullshit?"

"Big bull's shit. Bullshit. You do solve mysteries. You've solved a whole bunch of them since you moved here. I've watched you. I know. And nobody even wanted you to solve those mysteries. Now I'm handing you a mystery on a silver platter. I *want* you to solve one. You've got a case, Gladie. A case. A job. You can't say no."

"No."

"You don't want to get paid?"

My ears perked up like a puppy, and I might have mewed like a kitten. I was so seldom paid, that the idea of it got my whole body humming with expectation. "When you say, 'paid,' do you mean American money? Not that I'm opposed to any other kind of money."

"No. No money," she said, taking the keys out of the ignition. She held them up and swung them from side to side in front of my face.

"Are you trying to hypnotize me?"

"I think I was right about you being lobotomized. Don't you get it? They're keys. Car keys. My car keys," Ruth said.

"Your car keys?" I had no idea what she was talking about. And then suddenly I knew exactly what she was talking about. "Your car keys? Your car? You're going to pay me with your car?"

She nodded and continued to swing the keys in front of my face.

A car. I wanted a car so bad. I was still mourning the loss of my Oldsmobile Cutlass Supreme, and Ruth had the exact same car, except hers was in perfect shape. No rust. No ripped upholstery.

And actual keys to start the motor.

"I don't think so," I said. "I get along fine without a car."

I would have gleefully killed Ruth for her car, but I didn't want to steal from her. The truth was that I had solved a few mysteries since I had moved to Cannes, and I was more than a nosey parker buttinski when it came to mysteries. I was murder-curious, and normally I would have jumped at solving a murder, especially for a car. But this murder—if it was a murder—was pretty clear cut. Obviously, Ruth's sisters did the dirty deed, and Ruth was having a hard time coming to grips with it, even if she admitted that she suspected they were guilty. Since Ruth was meaner than spit, I wasn't going to be the one to break it to her that her sisters were on their way to the sieg heil pokey.

"You get along fine without a car?" she asked. "Like when you hitchhike, and a dog shoots the driver and hits the town's oldest tree and you become a pariah...again? Fine like that?"

She had a point. "You have a point," I said, buckling. Who cared if Ruth didn't like the outcome of the investigation? At least I would have a car, and I had to admit that nothing got my juices flowing more than a mystery. "Fine, but the investigation goes for no longer than seventy-two hours, and then if we haven't found the murderer or murderers, we call the cops. And you pay up front."

I put my hand out for her to drop the keys into it, but she put them in her purse, instead. "Okay to the seventy-two hours, because he's going to stink pretty bad by then, but payment is conditional on you solving the case."

"But..."

"Conditional on you solving the case," she repeated.

"What if you don't like the outcome?"

"I've lived through trickle-down economics. I can deal

with a little disappointment."

Ruth opened the glove compartment and took out two flashlights, handing me one of them. "Let's get started," she said. "Get your Miss Marple brain started. And don't wake up my sisters. I'll bet dollars to doughnuts they got Glocks under their pillows."

"Nixon," we said in unison.

Ruth got out of the car, but I was having second thoughts. Maybe a new car wasn't worth getting shot full of holes by two old ladies with Glocks. But I didn't want to get shown up by Ruth. If she was going to act brave, I wasn't going to wimp out in front of her. I gripped my flashlight tightly, and followed her up the porch steps. Ruth reminded me again not to wake up her sisters and opened the door quietly with her key.

Inside, we turned on our flashlights. We tiptoed through the parlor toward the window seat. "You open it," Ruth whispered.

"Are you chicken?"

"You're the detective. You open it."

Ruth's squeamishness gave me courage. I loved being the grown-up for once. Slowly, I opened the window seat and shined the light inside. Then, I closed it.

"Uh," I said.

"What? Did you find some clues?"

"Can you grow hair when you die?"

"What?"

"Hair? Can you grow hair?"

Ruth shined her light in my face. "Hair and nails grow for a little while, I think."

"That might explain it," I whispered. "Although…" I opened the seat and looked inside, again. "A full head of hair?"

"What are you talking about?" Ruth shined her light inside the seat.

"He was bald before, right?" I asked her.

"Yes."

"Looks like he's got a full head of hair now." With a trembling hand, I touched his hair and gave it a tug. "It's real," I whispered and wiped my hand on my sweatpants. "It also looks like he packed on the pounds since he died. He barely fits, now."

The man in the window seat was around the same age as Dwight Foyle, but he was rotund and hairy. He was wedged into the seat, taking up every square inch of it. I closed the seat cover.

"Ruth," I said gently. "I think this is a different guy."

"I know it's a different guy. I'm not blind. Maybe the other guy is in there, too?"

We searched for Dwight in the seat, but there was no sign of him. "Nope. Only the hairy, fat guy," I said.

We plopped down on the sofa and turned off our flashlights. Ruth dug in her purse and came out with a flask. She took a gulp and handed it to me. "What the hell is going on?" she asked. I didn't think she was asking me, and I didn't have an answer for her. I took a sip of the flask. It burned all the way down.

"This afternoon, we opened the seat, and it was the bald, skinny guy," she continued. "Now, it's the hairy fat guy."

"Both dead," I added.

"Both dead," she repeated.

She moved her hands, like she was directing a symphony. "Skinny guy. Fat guy. Same seat. Both dead."

"It's a lot," I agreed.

She ripped the flask out of my hand and turned toward me. "Well?" she demanded.

"Well?"

"Well? I hired you. Get on with it."

Strictly speaking, she had hired me to look into Dwight Foyle's death, and this was a totally different death. I wondered if she was going to pay me double, but I was too afraid to ask. "I guess the first thing to do is figure out who the hairy, fat guy is," I said, taking the flask from her again. I took a big gulp, ignoring the burn in my throat.

Ruth held both flashlights while I opened the window seat again. I dug my hand into his pocket to get his wallet, but he was wedged in so tight, his fleshy body folded in on itself, that once I got my hand in his pocket, I couldn't get it out again.

"It's stuck," I hissed.

"Come on, girl. Hurry up," Ruth whispered.

"I can't. It's stuck. My hand is stuck in the dead guy's pocket." The reality of the situation hit me, and I almost tossed my cookies. I began to panic. "Get it out. Get it out," I whispered to her.

Ruth put the flashlights under one arm and tugged at me with her other hand. Nothing. I didn't budge an inch.

"We're going to have to get him out of there or cut off your hand," she said.

"Really? Those are the only choices, Ruth? Geez, as

partners go, you're a real pip."

"We're not partners. I'm a client."

"Yeah, yeah, whatever. Help me get him out of here."

It took a lot of heave-ho'ing and every ounce of strength we had, but we finally managed to get the dead guy out of the window seat. Rigor mortis had set in, making him stuck in the same position he was in in the window seat. He was like a Popsicle, a rolled-up hedgehog. He hit the floor, rolled up, with a thud. I managed to extract my hand and his wallet with it. I held it up in triumph.

"It's probably not a good idea to look too closely at my life," I noted.

"You're telling me. So? Who is he?"

I opened the wallet and found his I.D. "Ross Tracy. Not Dwight Foyle. And Mr. Pants on Fire obviously lied about his weight to the DMV. Does the name sound familiar?"

Ruth rubbed her chin, like she was trying to remember. "No, and I haven't seen him around. There's a lot of old people around here, and they don't bother to come into town for tea."

But they did bother to come to Ruth's sisters' for tea. I let that thought stay with me for a moment. No use in beating Ruth over the head with the probability that she was related to crazy, psycho serial killers.

"Now what?" Ruth asked.

"I'm not CSI, Ruth," I complained, but I did give the body a once over. Just like Dwight, there was no sign of violence. Not even bugged out eyes or blue lips or anything hinting at violence.

He was just dead.

Was it possible that two men walked into this house and dropped dead of natural causes?

"It's like your sisters are friends with Putin or something," I told Ruth. "Do they have access to nuclear material?"

Ruth shined a flashlight onto my face. "I'm trying to figure out if you're serious or not."

I was totally serious. I had no idea how the two men died. "Of course, I'm not serious. Come on, let's stuff the guy back in the seat."

Getting him back in was significantly harder than getting him out. By the time we got the seat closed, we were sweaty and worn out. And hungry. "Is it weird that I'm hungry?" I asked.

Ruth nodded. "It's sort of weird. Yes."

"I guess I'm getting used to dead guys."

"I can see that. What's next?"

"We need to find Dwight," I said, like I really was Miss Marple. "He couldn't have gotten far, right? Ruth, if you were a dead guy, where you would hide in this house?"

"Contrary to popular belief, I'm not dead."

"Probably not far, right?" I asked again. "A closet?"

Ruth snapped her fingers. "Under the stairs," she breathed.

We shuffled our feet to the stairs, and Ruth opened the small door underneath. There, between various brooms, two bowling ball bags, and a bow and arrow set was Dwight Foyle, lying in a ball, as if he was still stuffed into the window seat.

Ruth and I exchanged looks, both of our mouths dropped open wide enough to store planes. "It's like it's the Cannes Cemetery annex or something," I said. "How many old men are we going to find if we keep looking?"

CHAPTER 7

Women chase men. Men chase women. Women chase women. Men chase men. Oy. Well, you get the picture, dolly. It's a free for all. But the question is: do all of these people really want who they're chasing? Sometimes we get so caught up in the hunt that we don't know why we're hunting. So, tell your matches to be careful what they wish for because they just might get it, and the getting it might be a pain in the tuchus. Like razor blade hemorrhoids for life.

Lesson 85, Matchmaking Advice from Your Grandma Zelda

Ruth didn't answer me. Her mouth was still open, and she was still staring into the closet under the stairs. I didn't think she was focusing on the bowling ball bags or the archery set. I didn't blame her. It was incongruous to say the least to have dead bodies hidden throughout the comforting, hospitable home. Corpses alongside comfortable furniture and handmade doilies was disorienting. I couldn't imagine how Ruth felt about her family home housing a bunch of dead guys.

"Goddamn Republicans," Ruth muttered and downed her flask, taking big gulps of the liquor. She handed it to me, but all that was left were a few drops.

"So, this isn't normal around here?"

Ruth grabbed the empty flask back, forcefully, and stuffed it into her purse. "Of course not. Who do you think we are?" she said but drifted off and looked up at the ceiling, as if she was re-thinking her entire existence. "I've never seen a dead body here, except when my mother died. Heart failure when she was one-hundred-and-five. My father died falling from a tree when he was picking apples, back before Serenity Village existed, when this was all apple orchards."

I patted Ruth's back. "I'm sure this is a new thing," I said, but I had my doubts. "Maybe they picked up a hobby late in life?"

It was a quiet moment, just us and the dead guys. That's what made it doubly terrifying when two shots rang out. It was an explosive noise; my heart beat so hard that I thought it would explode. Bullets sailed past our heads and into the wall behind us, sending at least a half dozen framed photos crashing to the floor.

"Hands up!" Ruth's sister Naomi shouted from the stairs.

"Make my day, punk!" Sarah shouted. Ruth's sisters were standing on the stairs, aiming their Glocks at our heads. I was so scared that my fight or flight response got overwhelmed, and I couldn't fight or flight. I stood paralyzed while my stomach threatened to hurl, and my pulse thought it was running the fifty meters at the Olympics.

"Put your glasses on!" Ruth shouted back.

"Huh? Huh?" Naomi and Sarah asked in unison.

Ruth grabbed the bow from the closet and brandished it like she was a Jedi warrior holding a lightsaber, sweeping it through the air and successfully knocking the guns out of her sisters' hands. Thinking quickly, I kicked the guns far away from us.

Once we were out of immediate danger, my knees buckled, and I collapsed to the floor. I put my head between my knees. "Thank God they weren't wearing their glasses," I said, trying to catch my breath.

"You almost killed us!" Ruth shouted. She continued to yell at her sisters, going into great detail about how voting for Nixon led to our almost demise.

"Ruth, is that you?" Sarah asked when Ruth finished.

"Are you back for the plumbing?" Naomi asked.

"You want some tea? I made fresh banana bread. Goes great with cream cheese," Sarah offered.

"I'll take some banana bread," I said between my knees.

They descended the rest of the stairs and walked toward the kitchen, but Ruth blocked them. She took a deep breath. "Do you have something to tell me?" Ruth had her authoritarian voice on high. It was her normal voice. She was a formidable presence, like Margaret Thatcher or a tank. I didn't think her sisters could deflect her line of questioning. "Huh? Something to tell me?"

"I didn't have walnuts to put in the banana bread, so I used pecans," Sarah admitted.

Ruth threw up her hands in frustration. "Get off the floor, girl. This is your job. You try to make some sense out of them."

I stood up. "Okay. Here it goes. Naomi, Sarah, did you notice anything different about the closet under the stairs?"

The four of us leaned over to get a really good look inside the closet. Mr. Foyle was still there, rolled in a stiff ball, and deader than a doornail.

"Oh, you mean Mr. Foyle?" Naomi asked. "He was a lot easier to move than poor Mr. Tracy. Mr. Tracy should have made better food choices."

I looked at Ruth. "There. I think that clears it up."

"What the hell is going on?" Ruth demanded.

"I think what Ruth means is, why are there two dead

men in your house?" I said.

"When it started, we thought Mr. Foyle was asleep. Isn't that so, Naomi?" Sarah asked.

"That's right," Sarah answered. "He was so peaceful in his chair, but we knew something was up pretty quick since he didn't snore."

"Mr. Foyle is a snorer," Naomi agreed.

"He just dropped dead while we were in the kitchen?" Ruth asked, gobsmacked.

"So we tucked him in the window seat with Mother's needlepoint cover on it," Sarah explained.

"As one does," I commented.

"He just dropped dead?" Ruth asked, again. She seemed relieved by this information, and I hated to pop her bubble.

"And poor Mr. Tracy dropped dead, too?" I asked.

"Wasn't that something?" Sarah said.

"Quite a coincidence," I noted.

"He came to visit this afternoon," Naomi explained. "We gave him a nice cup of tea. Sarah hadn't made the banana bread, yet, so he didn't eat that."

"Pity," Sarah said. "He did so enjoy my banana bread. It

would have been nice for him to go out with some of it in his stomach."

Naomi nodded, sadly. "And then all of a sudden, his eyes closed, and we thought: surely this one is just napping. But ten minutes later, we knew he was gone."

"So, we moved out Mr. Foyle and gave Mr. Tracy the window seat," Sarah said.

"In hindsight, that might have been a mistake," Naomi said.

Sarah nodded. "Like stuffing a cow into a chicken. Next time we'll grease them down."

"Next time?" Ruth asked. It was a good question. I had another good question.

"Why did you hide them?"

"Well, of course we hid them," Naomi said.

"Isn't that obvious?" Sarah asked.

"Obvious, right?" I asked Ruth.

"Shut up," Ruth told me.

Sarah closed the closet door, gently. "We couldn't have the world know. There would have been panic."

"Panic?" I asked.

"Because we opened a portal to hell," Naomi said, like we were five years old and she was explaining where poop came from.

"You got another flask?" I asked Ruth.

The four of us sat at the kitchen table, sipped tea, and ate banana bread. The banana bread was good, but the tea wasn't doing it for me. I was running on barely any sleep, and I needed one of Ruth's double-shot lattes.

"Gladie is going to look into this for a couple days and get to the bottom of it," Ruth said. Despite her age, she was in better shape than I was. Strong with an endless supply of energy. But sitting at the table, sipping tea, a few feet away from two dead men, Ruth seemed exhausted. Defeated. It was obvious that she wanted to hand off the entire debacle, even if she had to hand it off to me.

Sarah cut some more bread and focused on me. "We were thinking maybe you could bring Zelda over and close up the portal."

"The portal to hell?" I asked, as if there was another portal.

"Zelda can't do that. There's no portal to hell. The

Ouija board is a game, like Sorry or Monopoly," Ruth growled.

Sarah and Naomi didn't look convinced. I didn't blame them. If they weren't serial killers, then it was reasonable that they would try to come up with some explanation for why two men dropped dead in their home in a single day. Portals to hell was as good of an explanation as any. I was still not convinced that they weren't responsible, but I was willing to help Ruth out for a little while. I was also getting strangely attached to Naomi and Sarah, even if they had shot at me and voted for Nixon. They just didn't seem like they were systematically murdering the old men of Apple Serenity Village.

"My grandmother's gift doesn't extend to murder," I told them. "She only does love."

"Believe me, Gladie is the murder girl, not Zelda," Ruth insisted. "She's got a gift for it. She'll get this wrapped up in no time."

I blushed. I wasn't used to compliments and certainly not compliments from Ruth. I wasn't totally sure that being a "murder girl" was a gift, but Ruth seemed to think so.

Naomi looked worried. "Be careful, Gladie. You don't want to slip into the portal, too."

I shuddered. She was right. I didn't want to slip in the portal. "What's going to happen when people start looking for them?"

"They're not married, and their children are grown," Sarah explained.

"Just worry about finding the murderer," Ruth said.

It was a lot to ask. I had to figure out why two men died on the same day, and if they were murdered, who murdered them, and why. And I had to do it fast before their Mahjong partners or whoever noticed they were missing and before they started to stink, which I figured would be soon. Ruth was asking me to save her sisters. Me. The one who was responsible for a myriad of mishaps in town.

"I need a drink," I said.

Sarah put a bottle on the table. "Here. Mr. Foyle and Mr. Tracy enjoyed this."

Ruth and I locked eyes. I could almost hear the warning bells ding, ding, ding. "They both drank from this bottle today?" I asked.

They nodded, yes. "Gladie, you need to get the drink checked out," Ruth said, excitedly.

"Okay, Ruth. Take a sip, and we'll see if you drop dead. Look, I'm not CSI. Unless we turn it into the cops, there's no way to tell what's in that bottle." I gave a pointed look at her sisters. "But for now, nobody drinks it, okay?"

After our tea, Ruth's sisters decided to rope off the chair

where both men "slipped into the portal to hell." I wasn't sure a rope could block the devil, but I wasn't up on religion. I inspected the chair at a safe distance, just in case it was responsible for killing two men, but I couldn't see anything that would be responsible for their demise.

I pulled Ruth aside and asked her to drive me back into town. "I have to go to yoga with Bridget," I said.

"Now?"

"I know, right? Weird, flexible people like to torture themselves early in the morning, but what'cha gonna do? I promised Bridget I'd go to her prenatal class with her."

Ruth shook her head and crossed her arms in front of her. "No. I mean, *now*? Now when you have two murders to investigate? You have to stay here until you work it out."

"Here? With the dead guys and…" I leaned over and whispered into her ear. "And your sisters, who may or may not have killed them."

"They haven't killed you, yet, so I don't know what you're worried about."

"Ruth, they shot at me. I was inches away from having no brain, and don't joke about me not having a brain, anyway. I'm doing you a favor, remember?"

Ruth dug in her purse and came out with her car keys,

which she shook in front of my face. "Favor? Favor? Who's doing the favor?"

"I'm not sure a car is worth going to jail for being accessory after the fact." Oh my God. As the words flew out of my mouth, I realized that I could actually be prosecuted for murder. What was I doing? No, a car was *not* worth that.

"Oh, please," Ruth scolded. "Stop being dramatic. You'll find out who killed them. You'll be a hero, and the tree huggers will love you again, and so will the cop. That's what you want, right?"

The cop. I so wanted Spencer to love me. I wanted it more than I wanted a coffee, and I was jonesing pretty bad for a coffee. "I don't care if Spencer loves me, Ruth. I'm a modern woman."

She dropped the keys back into her purse. "You can go to yoga, but you have to come back to solve the murder. You can stay here for a couple days. I heard that Fred is tenting your house, anyway. You need a place to stay."

"I was planning on staying somewhere that wasn't, you know, the Psycho house."

Ruth ignored the Psycho reference and walked me to the front door. "Remember that Foyle was working on some secret, important story. He could have been murdered because of that."

Ruth handed me my coat and opened the front door. Sarah and Naomi came to the door to say goodbye. "Mr. Tracy was richer than Roosevelt," Sarah said. "Maybe the devil wanted his money."

"How rich is Roosevelt?" I asked.

"See you later," Ruth said. "I'll be in the shop in an hour or so." She sort of pushed me out of the door, and I grabbed onto her arm.

"Wait a minute. You're not driving me?"

"No. I have a couple things to do here before I go."

"So, how am I getting back to town?"

The old expression about never forgetting how to ride a bike is a total crock. That's what I was thinking, trying to ride away on Ruth's sisters' road. Ruth had gifted me her old bicycle, which had been housed in a shed behind the house for about thirty years. It took fifteen minutes to dig a path through the snow to the shed. Ruth pumped the tires with air, but the bicycle had seen better days, like when dinosaurs roamed the earth. I was worried about Ruth. The whole situation had taken a toll on her, and I had caught her staring at the snowdrifts behind the house, lost in thought. But Ruth wasn't a touchy-feely kind of person, and she wouldn't have welcomed me to comfort her there, behind the house. The best thing I could do for her was to get the murder mystery mess cleaned up as fast as I could.

Not that I thought I could clean it up. My mind went round and round, trying to figure out what I should do. Somehow, I had once again stumbled into a murder mystery. This time, though, I thought that Spencer should get involved. How could I leave two dead men, hidden away in an old house? They deserved dignity in death, not to be rolled up in a window seat.

On the other hand, I felt I owed it to Ruth to help out, and it was only for seventy-two hours.

But on the other, other hand, accessory to murder wasn't worth a Cutlass Supreme. And maybe I didn't even need a car. By the time I got to end of the road, the bike wasn't wobbling quite so much, and I was getting the hang of it. Maybe I could ride a bike everywhere, I thought. I would be in great shape, and Bridget wouldn't give me grief about polluting the planet and lining the oil companies' pockets with cursed pieces of silver.

It was bitter cold outside, but at least it wasn't snowing, and the plows had come through, clearing the roads and leaving tall walls of snow on both sides of the roads. As I turned onto the main road, I spotted the man who had run from Spencer the day before. He was skipping along with his deer. For some reason, I waved at him, and he waved back.

Even though I had had only a couple hours of sleep and not a drop of coffee, the fresh air felt wonderful, and it was fun to coast down the mountain, letting momentum move the bicycle. It was glorious to be in the countryside in the quiet, early morning, alone, just me and nature. The bike handled the road well, and I didn't even have to pedal. Why hadn't I gotten a bicycle sooner?

By the time I got back to the Historic District, I was a converted cyclist. I was determined to never take any other form of transportation. I no longer wanted a car. Ruth could keep her Oldsmobile. I even planned to buy a basket and bell for my new bicycle. Maybe I could paint it pink, too. That would look nice.

I turned onto Main Street where the town's oldest tree had toppled over. The memorial for the tree had grown exponentially since the middle of the night, and it was now guarded by two women dressed as trees.

I didn't care. I was no longer afraid about retribution, no longer afraid about revenge. I was now an environmentally-friendly commuter. I wasn't part of the problem; I was part of the solution. I was one with nature. Awake. Conscious. A one-woman windmill, solar panel, Prius. I waved at the tree huggers as I passed, and they waved their branches back at me.

'Cause they knew. They recognized my tree hugging

sisterness.

I loved my new bicycle! Despite the lawsuit and the dead men, I was positively euphoric. If I had known any songs about bicycles, I would have sung them.

A little ahead of me, the town's bus was driving toward me. "Look at that," I said out loud. "Len the bus driver is back from his gallbladder surgery."

I waved at Len, and he waved back. I could see his face through the bus windshield clearer, as he drove closer to me. He seemed as happy as I was. It was a magical morning, full of goodwill to mankind and trees. I had the sure feeling that nothing bad could possibly happen.

Then, Len drove over a patch of black ice.

I didn't believe what was happening at first. I mean, why would I? There was no reason to believe that a bus was going to lose control and careen toward me. Nope, I didn't believe it at all. That's why I didn't brake. But Len did. He braked, but the bus didn't care. It slipped and slid over the ice, unable to get traction, speeding up in a collision course with me and Ruth's ancient bike.

My survival instinct kicked in, and finally, I braked hard. So did Len. We made progress, slowing down considerably, and it looked like it would be a near miss, just a big scare to tell the grandchildren, if I ever had any. It all happened in a couple of seconds.

In slow motion, I watched as the bus inched forward, its wheels grinding to a halt, the bus sliding to the side, taking up the width of the road. Meanwhile, I managed to stop my bike, and I sat there on Main Street, watching the bus, as Len did everything he could not to kill me.

Just like with the truck and the tree the day before, the bus slowed down and just as it reached me, came to a full stop. And just like the truck and the tree the day before, it tapped me every so gently.

Gently for a bus, that is.

My bike went flying, and I went with it. For a crazy instant I thought, "Look! I'm flying!" But I quickly realized that I was actually falling. I swung my arms wildly, as if I was trying to catch my balance, mid-air. No luck. I shot through the air like a bullet from one of Ruth's sisters' guns.

I heard someone scream.

I think it was me.

I landed pretty quickly, face first in a snow bank. My head was wedged deep in the snow, and my lower half was sticking out of the snow bank. I was reasonably certain that I was still alive, but I wasn't completely sure. I stayed like that for about a minute while I tried to get my breathing under control. Also, I couldn't physically extract myself from the snow bank.

"Are you kidding me?" I heard, although the voice was muffled because of the snow.

CHAPTER 8

Who's in your bed, bubeleh? Who are you going all the way with? I mean, to death do us part all the way. This is something you have to think about when matching your matches. They will tell you about their type. Tall, short, fat, thin, brown eyes, blue eyes, likes jazz, likes hip hop. Whatever. I say feh to their type. Because this is the important thing: Types only last so long. Ditto sex, in most cases. But a best friend? A best friend is forever. Everyone needs a significant other who at least has the potential of becoming a best friend. With a best friend around, you're never alone and you're always supported. You're loved, and you're liked. You have someone to eat crackers in bed with and someone to go out in the middle of the night to get you crackers, if you don't have any. It might not seem important now, but ten years down the line, you'll turn to your sagging, wrinkled, smelly, leaves-the-seat-up fakakta husband and be the happiest woman in the world because you wound up with your best friend.

Lesson 46, Matchmaking Advice from Your Grandma Zelda

Spencer. He had a sixth sense whenever I humiliated myself. I kicked my legs to let him know I was still alive. He put his hand on my butt and gave it a little squeeze. Even with my head in the snow, my body heated up.

"Get your hand off my ass!" I yelled, but my voice was muffled from the snow so it didn't make much of an impact. With one tug, he pulled me out and clasped me around the waist, bringing me in close until our bodies were touching from toes to chins.

"Why Pinky, you really need to stop trying to get my attention. I'm more than happy to bring you to ecstasy without any preamble. No large vehicle needs to be involved."

"You're so funny that I forgot to laugh," I said. He had me so distracted that I had had to dig up a response from Junior High. His arms roamed down my back and then lower. I might have squirmed against him. He felt good against me. I almost forgot that I had been hit by a bus.

His lips touched my earlobe, kissing it gently. "You are such a troublemaker," he breathed into my ear. I shivered.

"I'm not a troublemaker," I moaned.

"Hey, you troublemaker!" someone yelled. I pushed away from Spencer. Len yelled at me through his window. "You're okay, right?"

"Well…" I started. I checked my body for protruding, broken bones. Miraculously, I was in one piece. "I guess I'm okay." By the time I got the words out, Len had put his bus into drive and was back on his route.

"I saw it happen," Spencer said. "I mean, I saw you flying through the air. You actually flew." His face lit up with excitement. "You even sped up midway, like you really had powers of flight. I think the arm waving slowed you down. Superman doesn't wave his arms, you know. You probably shouldn't do that next time. And the landing was dicey. Zero points for grace, there."

"Are you making fun of me? I could have died."

He grabbed me back to him. "Oh, Pinky. Of course I'm not making fun of you. Okay, maybe a little bit, but it's not every day I see my girlfriend flying through the air."

I leaned into him and rubbed the side of my face on his chest, like I was a cat. "You called me your girlfriend."

"It must be the stress. I meant to say my off-the-charts, kinky sex partner."

"I like that you're a cock-eyed optimist."

Spencer pointed. "Hey, look at that. A tree is riding a bike."

I turned to see what he was talking about. The bicycle that Ruth had just given me was being stolen, ridden off by one of the tree huggers. "That's my bike!" I yelled, pointing at the tree taking off with my bicycle.

"You have a bike?" Spencer asked.

"Ruth gave it to me. Go after the tree! The tree is stealing my bike!"

Spencer smoothed out his designer coat. "Pinky, I'm not chasing a tree. Yesterday, I chased after a man and his companion deer. I draw the line at a tree. It's just a bicycle. I have a reputation to uphold."

"But my bike."

He leaned in and gave me his best seductive face. "I'll make it up to you."

"I was hit by a bus, and a tree stole my bike," I said.

"And what does it say that I'm not even surprised anymore?"

I was peeved that Spencer wouldn't chase after the tree, but the truth was that I never want to see a bike again. If I had been driving Ruth's boat-sized Oldsmobile, I wouldn't have flown head first into a snow bank. From now on, my number one goal would be to solve the mystery and win Ruth's car. My moment of being one with nature was over. I would never wave at anyone again, and as far as I was concerned, the tree huggers could go straight to the portal of hell.

"Are you sure you're okay?" he asked, seriously. "Don't be courageous."

"I'm fine."

He ran his finger down the side of my face, making my toes curl. "Can you try to be more careful?"

"It wasn't my fault."

"At least you weren't chasing a murderer. It's a welcome change."

"Well," I said, giving him my best innocent expression.

"I'll pick you up at five, right?" he asked me. I had completely forgotten about our date. It would throw a wrench into the works with my investigation. But I didn't think I could get out of the date, and I couldn't tell Spencer about the dead men in Ruth sisters' house. Not yet, at least.

"Yes, but I'm staying somewhere else." I gave him the address after explaining about the bed bugs. He leaned over to kiss me, but we were interrupted by a car horn. My best friend

elise sax

Bridget drove up in her Volkswagen Bug. The passenger window opened.

"I heard that someone flew into a snowdrift," she called from the car. "I figured it was you. Are you ready for yoga?"

"Sure."

I said goodbye to Spencer and got into Bridget's car. She was wearing her usual hoot owl glasses and lots of blue eye shadow. With her pregnancy, her hair had grown fast, all the way to her shoulders. She was wearing yoga clothes, and she had a tiny belly from her growing baby.

"This is going to be good," Bridget said.

"Are you sure babies should do yoga?" I had never gone to a yoga class before. The skinny, put-together yoga chicks scared me. It was Bridget's first yoga class, too, but she seemed more confident about it than I was.

"It helps with bonding."

"You need that when you're pregnant?"

Bridget seemed to think about that for a moment. "I'm pretty sure. He needs to be fully bonded before I send him out into the world with a traumatic birth experience."

I shuddered. I didn't want to talk about a traumatic birth experience. "Do they sell coffee at the prenatal yoga place?"

"I've never been, but I think they have green juice."

Green juice wasn't coffee. "It's going to be fine, Bridget," I said because I thought Bridget didn't want to go to prenatal yoga any more than I did.

Pregnancy was hard. No alcohol and you had to exercise.

I loved prenatal yoga. At first I thought I was going to hate it, though. Bridget and I had entered the yoga studio, which smelled like incense, and the pregnant women were already there. Rich and thin…with mini basketballs protruding from their stomachs. It was like the Vogue Magazine version of pregnancy.

I didn't recognize one woman in the studio. They were all young, married, and probably hadn't been out of a relationship since high school. Definitely not Grandma's target clientele.

Neither the students or the teacher talked to us. Bridget and I looked out of place. I, for one, was wearing sweats and a t-shirt, what I had worn to bed. Bridget was wearing yoga pants and a "Margret Sanger is ashamed of you" t-shirt. We weren't exactly *Sex and the City*, like the rest of the class.

"I probably should have brushed my teeth for this," I whispered to her, as we rolled out yoga mats on the studio's wood floor.

Bridget looked around her, nervously. "I feel like I'm auditioning to be a mother, and I'm never going to get the part."

I gave her a hug. "You already got the part, sweetie."

We started by lying on our sides and taking slow, deep breaths. By the second breath, I was out.

Asleep.

I dreamed that I was sleeping with Mr. Foyle and Mr. Tracy. They were on either side of me on a king-sized waterbed. Each of them was rolled in a ball. I was on my back, looking up at the ceiling, which was a huge Ouija board. The Ouija planchette moved around on its own, spelling out: "Spencer is going to find out. You're in so much trouble. Don't forget to buy bagels."

From there, I floated away, flying without moving my arms like Superman to a large car dealership, where I looked at all the cars, but I couldn't open the doors because I didn't have a key. Finally, I went to Tea Time for my first free latte, but it was really poisoned tea, which forced me sing sitar music.

"We have to clear for the next class," I heard from far away. The dream faded, and I opened my eyes. I was back in the yoga studio, sitar music was playing softly from speakers, and a skinny, young yoga instructor was waking me up. Bridget was fast asleep next to me, snoring and drooling.

"What happened?" I asked, groggy. "When is the class starting?"

"You missed it," the yoga lady said. "In fact, it ended forty minutes ago. I let you sleep. Sometimes in your condition, you just need to sleep."

I sucked in my stomach and sat up.

"I would let you sleep through the next class, too, but you only paid for the one class," she continued.

I tapped Bridget on her shoulder, and she snorted. "Dehumanization of the masses!" she blurted out and sat up. "Where am I? What happened?"

"We fell asleep," I explained. Regular, non-pregnant yoga students started to file in. Bridget and I quickly gathered up the mats.

"Damn it. I wanted to bond," she complained.

"Maybe you did with the deep breathing."

Bridget didn't look convinced. We returned the mats to

the front desk and put on our coats. "I'm a terrible mother," she said and sniffed.

"That's not true. You care more about your baby than any mother I've ever seen, and your baby isn't even born yet."

"Really?" she sniffed.

"Really," I said, honestly. "How many other pregnant women worried that their unborn son has access to gender-stereotypical representations on television?"

She pulled me into a corner. "May I tell you something that I've never told anyone else?" she whispered. Her face was the picture of anxiety.

"Of course."

"I don't care about his access to gender-stereotypical representations on television. I want to binge watch *Friends* and eat S'mores Pop-Tarts. I don't want to care about bonding. I want to get a mani-pedi and read People Magazine."

It was like the weight of the world came off her shoulders, but she was still filled with guilt. I put my arm around her shoulders, and we walked to the front door. "Where are we going?" she asked.

"We're going to get mani-pedis and eat S'mores Pop-Tarts while we read People. But first we're stopping to get me a latte."

Ruth was working at Tea Time, just like every day, just like we weren't hiding two dead men a few miles away. She threw me a look that could kill, making it pretty clear that I was supposed to act normal, too.

"Latte, please, Ruth," I said at the counter, winking twice and smiling. I couldn't wait for my first free latte. It was like winning the lottery.

"I'd like an herbal tea, but I need royal jelly to put in it. Do you have royal jelly?" Bridget asked.

Ruth furrowed her brows. "What are you, some kind of hipster? Where's your knit cap and beard? No skinny jeans? Royal jelly. Royal jelly? You want a vegan, gluten-free Cronut to go with your royal jelly?"

"That sounds kind of good, Ruth. Sure, I'll take a vegan, gluten-free cronut," Bridget said. She was never much for reading a room. Ruth walked away in a huff, and I figured I wasn't going to get my first free latte, today.

"How about we go to lunch before mani-pedis?" I suggested to Bridget. She jumped at an offer for a full meal. We called our friend Lucy to join us at Saladz, and we walked the block to the restaurant.

Saladz was a popular café. There was a large area to eat outside, but that was closed, because of the cold. Bridget and I took a seat in the center of the restaurant next to Jose and two of his friends, who were still dressed as miners.

Jose waved when we took a seat, and I introduced him to Bridget. "How's the play coming along?" I asked.

"It's not a play. It's an homage to the founding of our town. An embodiment of our soul. But that soul is in jeopardy. We must let truth win out so that justice will prevail."

Bridget's ears perked up, and she smiled big. She looked happier than she had been in weeks. "Justice?" she asked. "You're looking for justice?"

Bridget spent her whole life looking for justice for everyone from apple pickers to circus elephants. Her weeks spent making the perfect baby had drained her and had distracted her from her life-long pursuit.

Jose told Bridget what he claimed was the true story of Cannes's founding. He explained that a former Confederate soldier and slave-owner came out west and founded the town with ill-gotten gains, money off the backs of enslaved people.

Bridget's mouth dropped open. "We have to fight this." I got the impression that she was talking more to herself than to anyone else. She had a purpose. "The founder's play can't go on as normal."

"We're protesting at the rehearsal in an hour," Jose told her.

Bridget turned toward me. "Is it okay if we postpone the mani-pedis?" Her face was glowing with the prospect of protesting local, amateur actors.

"Of course," I said.

"Darlins', what a day! What a day!" Our southern belle friend Lucy Smythe exclaimed, making an entrance into Saladz. She was wearing a long fur coat and fur hat, and she was perfectly made up. "Faux fur, darlin'," she told Bridget, as she took a seat. "I saw those daggers shootin' out of your eyes."

She shrugged her coat off and put the hat on the table. "How are my buddies?"

"Gladie flew, and I'm going to protest our founding fathers," Bridget explained, excitedly.

"I'm so happy for you," Lucy told Bridget. "It's like you've gotten your groove back. We should celebrate."

"Oh, yes," Bridget said. "I'm going to get a Monte Cristo sandwich and fries. Oh, and a milkshake!"

Lucy patted her hand. "That's the Bridget I know and love." She turned toward me. "You flew? Did it have something to do with the tree huggers?"

"No, the tree huggers were when her dog shot the trucker," Bridget answered for me.

"Strictly speaking, it wasn't my dog."

"Of course it wasn't," Lucy said. We ordered lunch, and the waiter served our drinks. Bridget got a milkshake, and Lucy and I got iced tea. Lucy squeezed lemon into her drink and stirred. "Well, I've been busy, too. Looking for a diamond for my engagement ring."

"Doesn't the man do that?" I asked.

"Gladie, if you're a very dumb woman, then yes, you let the man do that. But I'm not dumb. So, I'm looking for a big diamond. Big. Hope Diamond big."

"We get the picture, Mrs. Trump," I said.

"I just drove in from Los Angeles. Nothing there. I'm going to have to expand my search parameters."

"Be careful that you don't get a blood diamond," Bridget instructed. "That would be tragic."

"Don't worry about me. My diamond will be flawless."

Lucy was getting married to Uncle Harry in a month on Valentine's Day. Uncle Harry wasn't her uncle or anyone else's as far as I could tell. He was a retired businessman, and I got the impression his business was the shady kind. Lucy worked in marketing, whatever that was, but had more or less stopped working since Uncle Harry proposed. A month wasn't long to plan a wedding, but Lucy didn't seem concerned about the logistics. Money sure made difficult things easier.

After lunch, Bridget followed her new cause to rehearsal protests, and Lucy agreed to drive me home to pick up my things. Outside, the tree huggers were picking up trash from the street.

"I do like how the tree huggers have been sprucing up the place," Lucy said. "Get it? Sprucing? Cause they're trees? Anyway, normally we get wackos who are mean. Like the cult or the ones who loved snakes, but these wackos are nice. I wouldn't mind if the tree huggers stayed around for a while."

She had a point. They were pretty mellow for being angry, and there wasn't a peep out of them about seeking revenge against me. But they did steal my bike. "I hear they're going to plant a thousand trees, you know, because of the old tree you knocked down."

"I didn't actually knock it down. You see, this dog…"

Lucy clutched my arm tightly. "Oh, for the love of Dixie. Are you seeing that?"

I followed her gaze to Bird's hair salon. Three women dressed head to toe in black outfits with black knit caps, like they were jewelry thieves, looked both ways and then skulked into the shop.

"What the devil is that?'" Lucy asked.

"Maybe they're having bad hair days."

"Or maybe they want to rob the store, steal the permanent solutions. Or the curlers. Or maybe some scissors? Oh, I guess not."

I had a feeling about what they were doing at Bird's, but I didn't feel like explaining to Lucy that Bird had transformed herself into Radan the Horrible in order to get more thigh gap.

"So, explain to me again what we're picking up from your place?" Lucy asked, beeping her car unlocked.

I got in the passenger seat. "Enough clothes for three days, and an outfit for my date." I added the last part under my breath.

"Your what?"

"My date."

"With Spencer, right? Or did someone new come to town?"

"With Spencer. My date's with Spencer. I'm not a whore," I said.

Lucy stuck her fingers up, like she was pinching an

inch-worth of air. "Well, maybe a little one."

She had a point, up to a point. Since moving to town, I had been involved with three men, but I had only had sex with one of them. Spencer was the big one I had been waiting for. The whale. "Well, those days are over. Now, it's just Spencer and me."

"So, that's why you have that look."

"What look?"

"The look like you're about to catch something, darlin'. I'm not talking about herpes. I mean, you've got your hunting face on."

"I don't have a hunting face."

"Sure you do. You've got it right this second. But usually someone's got to drop dead, first. Oh my God! Someone's dropped dead!"

CHAPTER 9

A lot of people come to me, and they say, Zelda, why do you always look so nice. Have you noticed, bubeleh, how nice your bubbe looks? I mean, I'm no Audrey Hepburn, don't get me wrong. But I never put on any old shmata. When I'm out in the world, I dress like I'm a queen. A queen. So, I found a lovely man named Shel, who makes me whatever I want. He's a dynamo wizard with a needle and thread. If I want to dress like Barbra Streisand, he says, no problem. Princess Diana? Simple. Why do I go through the trouble of dressing nicely every day, even though I'm not a vain person? Why do I wear pantyhose when I believe that beauty is in the eye of the beholder? It's because my philosophy is, "Be the person you want to be." You got it, dolly? You understand? Years ago, I met a nice young man—his name was Dalai something—and he told me to start from where you are. He told me that the Buddha said that. It sounded good to me because we keep waiting to be rich, thin, stylish, and Audrey Hepburn before we allow ourselves to live. No good, bubeleh. You need to dress the part, be the person you want to be. Start now. Don't wait. If your heart tells you that you are a cowboy, slip on those boots. If your heart tells you that you're Hillary Clinton, buy yourself a pantsuit. You know, the Buddha was a smart guy. I think he was Jewish.

Lesson 19, Matchmaking Advice from Your
Grandma Zelda

I tried to change my face, but I couldn't do it. Damn, my hunting face. But Lucy knew me too well. While I should have been thinking about my date with Spencer, I had been really thinking about the two dead guys, who were rotting at Ruth's sisters' house. I was gripped by the mystery. Were they murdered, or could it have been a crazy coincidence that they died in the same spot on the same day? Naomi and Sarah said they hid the bodies because they didn't want to spread panic about the portal to hell, but were they lying? And how would Ruth take it if her sisters turned out to be serial killers?

There was another possibility, which is what probably gave me the hunting face. That possibility was that there was a killer preying on people in the Apple Serenity Village. He had already killed twice. What if he killed again before I discovered who he was? I had promised Ruth that I wouldn't tell a soul about the deaths, but it wasn't a responsible promise. I owed it to Mr. Foyle and Mr. Tracy to tell Spencer about it. Leave it to the cops.

But I had promised Ruth. And it was only for seventy-two hours.

And I was going to get a car.

"Nobody's dropped dead," I said. "I'm just nervous about my date."

Lucy turned the car onto my grandmother's street. "Your eye twitched!"

elise sax

"No, it didn't," I said, touching my eye.

"Now, the other one is twitching!"

She parked on the street in front of the house and turned off the motor. "Was it Ruth? I figure it's only a matter of time before someone kills that woman."

"Ruth's still alive. She was yelling at Bridget an hour ago."

Lucy touched her chin and looked up at the car's ceiling. "The mayor? The taco man? Oh, come on, Gladie. Spit it out. The list is way too long for me to guess. Listen, I love planning my wedding, but I need a little more in my life to keep me interested. Help me out. Give me a murder."

She batted her eyelashes at me, but I clapped my hand over my mouth, refusing to say a word. Since begging didn't work, Lucy resorted to violence. She pinched my arm as hard as she could, and even through my coat, it sent a shockwave of pain through me. I slapped her hand away and rubbed my arm.

"Okay. Okay. There may be a little murder," I said.

"Oh, girl, you could never be a spy. You give it all up because of a pinch."

"It was a big pinch," I complained.

"So, who was murdered, and when do we start

investigating?" If I had a hunting face, Lucy had a euphoric face. She loved mysteries.

"I can't tell you. It's top secret."

I opened the car door and stepped out. With the talk about murder, I hadn't noticed that the house was now covered with a tent.

Lucy trotted around the car and hopped onto the sidewalk. "What do you mean, 'top secret?' You mean like the CIA?"

"I can't tell you, and don't pinch me, again. And no, not like the CIA." I pointed my finger at her nose. "Don't say a word to anyone. To anyone. You understand?"

She nodded. "I could do that. I mean, if we can make a deal that I like."

Me and my big mouth. Lucy had me over a barrel. Why couldn't I keep a secret? I walked up the driveway, and Lucy followed. Guilt overwhelmed me because I had forgotten about Grandma. I hadn't helped her at all at a time when she was losing her home for three days. It would be a huge change and trauma for her, and I should have been there to help her make the transition. She had said she was willing to live in a tent in the backyard, but I didn't think she could handle it. She was used to her house, not a flimsy tent outside in the middle of winter.

I walked through the side gate, passing a cable guy. At the back of the house, other workers were coming and going, and in the center of the backyard was a large mobile home. "What the hell?" I said.

"Now, this is what I call camping," Lucy gushed.

We walked toward the trailer. Workers had attached various wires and pipes. Fred was still handling the tent of poison on the house. "Hello, Underwear Girl! I'm pumping in a double dose! Nothing's coming out alive," he called. He was thrilled at the prospect of dead bugs, but he didn't inspire confidence as he fought with the tent.

"This is like being back stage at Armageddon," Lucy said. A big smile was plastered on her face, like this was the most fun she had ever had. I knocked on the trailer's door, and Meryl, the blue-haired librarian, answered.

"Oh, hi. Your grandmother and I were just watching *Ballers*. I love your 4K."

"What's a 4K?" I asked. We walked inside. A 4K was a television, and this one was gigantic. It was framed in gold. Underneath, there was a roaring fire in the fireplace. "There's a fireplace?" I asked, looking at the fireplace.

"Take a seat," Meryl urged, sitting on the sectional. "It's got dual massage settings." Grandma was laid out on the sectional, clutching the remote in her hand.

"I like the vaulted ceilings," Lucy said.

Something dinged. "That must be the popcorn," my grandmother explained.

"I'll get it," Lucy said. The kitchen bordered the living in one great room. "I love the marble counters," she called.

"Where did you get this?" I asked my grandmother.

"Word got out that I was homeless. A nice man in Omaha, Nebraska sent it over, just until the bugs are gone. I matched his daughter. Lovely woman."

"Omaha? A nice man from Omaha sent you over a luxury mobile home? Who was it? Warren Buffett or something?"

She pointed at me. "That's the one. Nice man."

Lucy came back in with a large bowl of popcorn. "Zelda, you've got foie gras and caviar in the refrigerator."

"Does that go well with popcorn?"

"Darlin', that goes well with everything."

"Wasn't it nice of Mr. Buffett to stock the mobile home? Egyptian cotton sheets on the bed, too," Grandma said.

"I'm having so much fun. We're having a party," Meryl said, taking the bowl of popcorn from Lucy. "We're going to binge watch all of the Patrick Swayze movies. I sure like his ass. Especially in *Road House*. Hubba. Hubba."

"Look at the coffee table. Is that mahogany?" Lucy asked.

A commercial started on the television, and my grandmother stood up and stretched. "Dolly, I packed you a bag. I put in a date dress, too, and here." She approached and handed me a dozen condoms.

"Oh, that looks promising," Lucy said.

"What's this?" I asked.

"Has it been that long?" Lucy asked. "All right, I'll tell you. You see, when two people are in love..."

I put my hand up. "Okay, smarty-pants, I recognize what they are. I just want to know why she's giving them to me."

But I didn't need to ask. If my grandmother was giving them to me, it meant she thought that I was going to need them. The condoms got my hopes up. Sure, I was in the middle of a murder mystery. Sure, I was homeless because my bed was infested with bed bugs. Sure, I needed to be certain if I really was in a committed relationship with Spencer before I had sex with him.

But sex with Spencer! Oh, goody!

"A dozen condoms?" I asked Grandma. A dozen times seemed just about right. I might need Advil, after, but no pain no gain.

"I'm picking up a lot of heat, bubeleh. But I can't be sure it'll be tonight. You might have to wait a while."

"A lot of heat is good."

"Just like a boy scout," Lucy said. "Always prepared."

I slipped the condoms into my purse and got my bag from the bedroom. It occurred to me that I could leave Ruth in the lurch and sleep in the luxury trailer instead of the house of horrors, but a deal was a deal. Besides, the trailer was going back to Omaha in three days, and I wanted a car.

I kissed my grandmother goodbye, but before Lucy and I could leave, the trailer's door burst open and the three women dressed as cat burglars walked in. They looked like they had been through a war. Their clothes were torn, and one of them had a black eye.

"Zelda. Zelda," one of them moaned and plopped down on the couch. She put her head in her hands. "It was terrible."

"The apocalypse," another woman in black cried.

"I told you this wasn't the way," Grandma said. "Bird needs to decide on her own to be brought out of it. Three friends trying to deprogram her won't work."

"But she's in deep," the first woman said. "Real deep. She kept calling herself Radan the Horrible, and she had superhuman strength."

"She broke a table with her hand, and it didn't hurt her a bit," the third woman announced. "Then she cackled like a witch and said she had to banish us from her kingdom."

"And she did," the first woman said, haunted. "She really did."

"What's going on?" asked Lucy.

"Bird's on a new diet," I explained.

"Oh, it must be really strict."

I wondered if I should stick around and help my grandmother. Handling three would-be deprogrammers was going to throw a wrench in the works of her party. "Go ahead, dolly," she said, like she had read my mind. "I got this."

I was relieved to be set free. I wasn't in the mood to handle Radan the Horrible. Lucy and I walked outside. "Hello, Underwear Girl," Fred called. He was fiddling with the tent. He didn't look very good.

"You look green, Fred."

"That's normal. Dangerous job, but someone's got to do it. Look, Mickey Mouse is dancing with Pluto."

His eyes rolled into his head, and he stumbled backward. "You okay?" I asked.

"Timber!" Lucy called.

I put my hands out to catch him, but who was I kidding? No way could I catch a grown man. Fred fell backward, flat as a board. He hit the ground

"That's not the murder, right?" Lucy asked.

"He's not dead. Oh, Fred, you're not dead, right?" I crouched down and felt for a pulse. His heart was beating, and he was breathing, but he was out cold. "Fred, wake up. Fred." I slapped his cheek, gently, and he came around.

"Wow, you're pretty. You're like a sunset but soft, and you smell good."

I was still wearing my pajamas, and I hadn't brushed my teeth in almost twenty-four hours. I was reasonably sure that I didn't smell good, but I was soft. "Fred, what happened?"

"I don't know. I might have gotten a lung full of the bed bug poison. I should have known something was wrong when John Lennon delivered me a pizza."

"Fred, maybe you should let someone else do the exterminating thing, and you could go back to being a policeman. I think being shot at would be less dangerous."

Fred sniffed. "Oh, Underwear Girl, you don't know how good that sounds. I would love to be shot at. Criminals don't give me the willies like bugs do. But I can't go back to the job I love. I let them down."

"Oh, Fred," I said because I couldn't think of anything else to say. I hated to see him like this, despondent and half-poisoned. But I was up to my armpits in emergencies, and Fred was going to have to wait.

"The tent looks great, Fred. I think it's time for you to go home now."

"You think that would be all right?"

"I do."

Lucy and I helped him up and into his Kill the Critters truck.

"Your life is exhausting," Lucy said, when Fred drove off. "I don't know how you do it every day."

"I carbo load."

"Still, carbs don't make you bulletproof. Speaking of bulletproof, when are you going to tell me about the murder?"

Spencer was going to pick me up in two hours, and I couldn't get into it with Lucy. She was like a dog with a bone whenever I discussed murder with her. She would be all over

Ruth's sisters' house, looking for more corpses, if I told her now. So, I arranged for her to pick me up the next morning.

"Eight in the morning," I said. "We can get coffee first, and then you can help me do some snooping."

Lucy's face brightened. "I love snooping. Should I bring a gun? A cattle prod?"

I thought about that for a moment. "I'm hoping we won't need weapons."

"Darn it."

Lucy dropped me off at Ruth's sister's house and thank goodness, didn't ask to be let in. I rang the doorbell, and Naomi answered. She was wearing another Jackie Kennedy suit. This time, it was blue.

"Ruth? Is that you, again?"

"No, it's me. Gladie."

She grabbed my arm and gave it a tug inside. "I think we have a problem," Naomi said, adjusting her pillbox hat with great concern.

"Another one or the same one?"

"I think the portal of hell is growing."

That didn't sound good. "When you say, growing, do

you mean another man dropped dead?"

Sarah walked in from the kitchen. She was wearing overalls and a frilly shirt, again, and she was coated in a light dusting of flour. "Did you tell her about the portal?" Sarah asked her sister.

"I was just about to. Look, Gladie."

She pointed at the chair. It looked exactly how it looked in the morning. It was big and comfortable-looking. Overstuffed with a doily laid over the back. Then, I saw it. "Where did the rope go?"

"Where did the rope go?" Naomi repeated, like she was hosting a new season of *The Twilight Zone*.

"It must have been sucked down," Sarah said. "Sucked into the portal."

I clutched my bag to my chest and took a deep breath. Could the portal to hell be real? Sarah gave me a little push. "Go ahead," she said. "Use your powers. Check it out."

"My powers are highly overrated. Maybe we should wait for a professional." Like the police.

"You're the professional," Naomi insisted, giving me a push, too.

I put my bag down and took off my coat. I took another

breath for courage and approached the chair. It looked completely normal, like it hadn't been the scene of two murders. Walking around it, I gave it as wide of a berth as possible. I couldn't see anything out of the ordinary.

"Are you sure you didn't take the rope off? Maybe used it for something else?" I asked. The sisters shook their heads.

"The portal, Gladie," Naomi said. "It's alive."

I shuddered and took two steps away from the chair. "Maybe we should move the chair outside," I suggested.

"Go ahead," Sarah said. "Move it."

I wasn't going to touch the chair. I didn't believe in portals to hell, but I wasn't going to touch the chair. "On second thought, maybe we should leave it there so that we don't make the portal bigger."

"Oh, good point," Sarah said. "I told you she had Zelda's gift," she told her sister.

"I hope you can close the portal before word gets out," Naomi said, wringing her hands.

Sarah agreed. "There would be a panic. Like double-coupon day at the Mini-Mart."

The grandfather clock chimed four times. I had an hour to get ready for my first date with Spencer. "Maybe the rope thing was a fluke," I said. "Can I investigate later? I have a date."

"Oh, a date," Naomi said, a big smile growing on her face. "I love those. Going to the picture show? Or maybe out for a malted?"

"I think he's taking me out for dinner. He'll be here soon. Did Ruth tell you that I'm staying for a couple days?"

"Did Ruth tell us that, Sarah?"

"She told us to give her Ruth's room, remember?"

"That's right," Naomi said. "You'll want fresh towels, of course. Follow me."

Ruth's childhood bedroom was on the third floor, in a turret at the back of the house. It occurred to me, standing in it, that no one could hear me scream from way up there. The back of the house looked out to the remaining woods that the Apple Serenity Village hadn't taken over. Snow was everywhere. I wasn't sure that Cannes had ever seen so much snow, but the grounds were covered in feet of it, and the trees were covered like frosted cookies.

Ruth's room was simple, with a brass bed and quilt. Next to it, a nightstand and lamp. There was an old-fashioned bowl and pitcher on a wooden chest of drawers. Naomi opened an antique wardrobe and pulled out a couple of towels.

"Bathroom's two doors down," she explained. "It takes a while for the hot water to reach up here, but once it gets here, it's good and hot." She studied my face for a moment. "Are you gonna have sex tonight? An under the cover rumble?"

I was hoping for an under the cover rumble.

"It's just a date. A first date," I explained.

"So, he's got a small pecker, then? You can do a lot with a small pecker, unless it's really small like a hummingbird. Then, you can't do much. But a robin-sized pecker will do the job."

"I don't know much about birds."

"Oh, that's a shame." She walked toward the door. "Take your time getting ready," she said, walking away from me. "A little witch hazel should handle that pimple on your chin."

I slapped my hand over my chin. She was right. There was a big zit, there. Just perfect. And who the hell was Witch Hazel?

I took a bath because there wasn't a shower. Thankfully, my grandmother had thought to pack all of my makeup and toiletries. She even packed my best panty and bra set. I used everything in my arsenal to make me as drop-dead, impossible to forget, gorgeous for my date with Spencer. We were starting something, and I wanted it to be perfect.

My grandmother had packed a bright red dress for me. It had a tight bodice with spaghetti straps and flared out below to mid-thigh. I was going to freeze, and my toes in the strappy four-inchers that Grandma packed for me were going to get frostbite and have to be cut off.

But I looked hot.

By the time I got finished getting ready, it had grown dark, and the house was filled with spooky shadows. It dawned on me that I was going to have to sleep in a house with two dead bodies and possibly their murderers. I double-checked that the condoms were in my purse. Maybe I would get lucky with Spencer and sleep at his place instead of the house of horrors.

I walked carefully down the stairs in my high heels. I could hear Naomi and Sarah talking to someone downstairs. When I reached the bottom floor, I saw who they were speaking to.

Spencer had arrived early, and he was staring at the portal to hell.

CHAPTER 10

And then it happens. You know what I'm talking about, bubeleh? The date. The first date. How do you young people call it? The big Kahuna. I'm not talking about just any first date. I'm talking about the first date that your match wants. The golden ticket first date. The Emerald City first date. The first date with Hugh Jackman, you know, if he wasn't married and you could match someone with him. Anyway, after all that, I'm not talking about the actual first date. I'm talking about the before the first date. Not the waxing, manicure, or buying the new dress before the date. I'm talking about the time to relax. Reflect. The calm before the storm. A bissel of meditation or a small Xanax. You'll probably have to talk your match down, make him or her breathe and take a step back to get in touch with themselves before they take the big step to coupledom. You'll see a lot of vomiting and crying. It comes with the job.

*Lesson 58 Matchmaking Advice from Your
Grandma Zelda*

Spencer looked good. Real good. Like the world's sexiest man, but sexier. He was dressed in Armani, which fit him perfectly. He dressed in black, which reflected the color of his lush hair and made his blue eyes stand out. His face was cleanly shaved for once, and I could smell his aftershave from the staircase.

Yum.

I was glad he was wearing cologne to cover any smell of decomposition from the two hidden dead men. But I was terrified that he was in the house, only feet away from them. I had planned to meet him outside, or at very least, block him at the door, but Ruth's sisters had let him into the house, and now he was staring at the fateful chair.

The portal of hell chair.

"Gladie, look who's come to visit," Naomi said, obviously delighted.

Spencer looked me up and down and arched an eyebrow. I could see his pupils from across the room. Big. Aroused. My body heated under his gaze. I felt incredibly sexy, suddenly, and I slinked the rest of the way to him, my body lithe like a cat in heat.

As I got closer to him, the chemistry between us combined, stirring into something combustible. I realized that I was panting, and I took a deep breath.

"Spencer," I said.

"Gladie." He used my real name, instead of his nickname for me, and his voice was deeper than normal. I shivered at the sound of it.

"Definitely not a hummingbird," Naomi whispered as I walked by her.

"Please take a seat," Sarah told Spencer. "Visit for a minute before you two leave for your date."

"I'd love to," he said but never took his eyes off me.

I pushed my lips together, holding back a strong desire to growl and pounce on him like a lion. Oh, yes. Grandma's condoms were getting used tonight.

Spencer moved to take a seat, but he picked the portal to hell. As he crouched above it, Ruth's sisters and I shouted in unison, "No!"

Spencer popped up in surprise. Sarah caught him first, putting her arm around his waist. "Not there, honey," she said. "We're getting it re-covered."

"Oh. Sorry."

"Naomi, let's get the lovebirds some tea,' Sarah said.

"We're about to leave," Spencer explained.

Naomi smiled. "It won't take a minute."

When they left, Spencer took my hand and brought it to his lips. "You're stunning tonight, Pinky."

"Oh," I moaned. His lips were hot and strayed a moment on my hand, sending shockwaves of want and desire through me. I was like a bulimic at a tour of Ben & Jerry's.

"Come on. Let's take advantage of our minute alone."

He steered me across the room. Since I was stunned by the overload of hormones rushing through me, I didn't realize at first that we were walking toward the window. Spencer sat down on the window seat and patted the space next to him. "Come on, Pinky. Let's make out."

"Uh," I said, staring at his crotch, which was on top of poor, dead Mr. Tracy.

"What's the matter?" Spencer asked. "Don't tell me you changed your mind."

"Uh…"

He smirked his annoying little smirk and arched an eyebrow. I loved when his eyebrow did that, and I wondered what other body part he could raise at will. "Oh," I moaned.

"There she is," he said, never taking his eyes off of me. Spencer's voice was low and gravelly, deep and seductive. His fingers trailed up my arm, making my insides melt. His hand curved around my arm and pulled me close. "Come and sit, Pinky. Let me drive you wild."

I so wanted him to drive me wild, but not on a dead man. My eyes shifted to the seat, again.

"What? What is it?" he asked. He looked down at the spot next to him. "Something wrong with the seat?" He began to inspect it.

"No. No. Nothing wrong with the seat." I tried to smile to drive my point home, but I couldn't. I was too freaked out. "Come on over here," I said. The portal to hell was better than him discovering that he was sitting on dead Mr. Tracy.

"What are you playing at? What's wrong?" Spencer was giddy, like we were playing hide and seek or some other game. He looked down at the seat next to him, again. "Are you hiding something from me, Pinky?"

"No?" I said like a question. I was having trouble breathing. I wracked my brain, trying to come up with something to distract him, but all I could think of was "look over there!" and I didn't think that would work.

As if in slow motion, I watched Spencer get up and look down at the seat. His hand touched its edge and slowly, he opened it. I closed my eyes and stopped breathing. Even my heart stopped. I was more or less dead. Even so, my brain was going a mile a minute. It was thinking about how I was going to look in orange and shackles. It was thinking how my night of passionate, hot, sweaty snuggle-bunnies was going to be snatched away from me, and how Spencer would be so angry at me that he would never shave for me again.

He opened the seat and looked inside.

"It's not what it looks like," I blurted out. "I mean, it is, but it isn't. You see, hell really exists, and Cannes looks innocent and all, but, well, I wanted to tell you, but I couldn't. I mean, I could have, but I said I wouldn't. And, well..."

"Huh," Spencer said, shrugging. He closed the seat. "Nothing in there. I could have sworn you were hiding something from me."

"What are you talking about?"

"You had me there for a moment. I was sure you were hiding something. Come on and sit next to me."

I pushed him out of the way and opened the seat. Nothing. There was nothing there. Not Mr. Tracy. Not Mr. Foyle. Not even a button. It had been completely cleaned out. I ducked my head inside and looked closer. "There's nothing in here," I announced from inside the window seat. "Not a thing. Nothing. There's nothing in here."

Spencer pulled me out of the window seat. "You okay?"

I pointed to the chair and then the window seat and then back at the chair. "Nothing," I said, pointing again to the seat and then the chair. I grabbed his shoulders. "The portal of hell," I breathed.

"Is this the kinky part of the evening? I was hoping for something involving lace and page fourteen of the Kama Sutra, but you know, I'm pretty much game for anything." He put his arms around my waist and pulled me close. "God, you're a beautiful woman, do you know that?" His breathing slowed, and he studied my face, like he was trying to memorize it. Then, he swallowed, hard. "So, what do you want me to do? Role play? You said, portal of hell? You want me to be the devil, and you can be an angel. Naked angel, of course."

I blinked. "What did you say?"

"Here we are," Sarah announced, as she and Naomi walked back in, pushing their tea cart. "I made a peach cobbler that'll knock your socks off, but I don't want to spoil your appetite for dinner."

Spencer let me go. "The tea smells great."

"English Breakfast, even though it's not breakfast time," Naomi said.

Behind Spencer's back, I pointed at the window seat and put my palms up in question to Ruth's sisters.

"There's nothing in the window seat," Naomi said,

answering my silent question. I slapped my forehead. Ruth's sisters sucked at lying.

"We know," Spencer said. "We checked." I pointed at the closet, but Spencer turned around and caught me. "What's going on?" He looked at the closet. "I knew it. I knew you were hiding something."

He walked toward it. I ran around him and blocked him with my arms outstretched at my sides. "Pinky, your secret is out. I'm going to look in the closet. What did you get me?" He kissed me lightly. "It's very sweet of you to get me a birthday present. And three days early. Very sweet."

I had had no idea that it was almost his birthday, and I hadn't gotten him a thing. I dropped my arms, and he walked around me. In a matter of seconds, he was going to open the closet, and he was going to know that not only didn't I get him a birthday present, but I hid a dead body from him.

Hearing the closet door open behind me, I turned around. Spencer was looking inside it.

"It's not what you think," I said.

"True. I thought you were going to get me soap on a rope."

I dropped my head in shame. "I'm sorry I didn't get you soap on a rope."

"Don't worry, Pinky."

I waited for the blowup, but it didn't come. No shouts of "What the hell!" or anything. I shot a look at Naomi and Sarah, but they were busy pouring tea, unconcerned that Mr. Foyle was about to be discovered in the closet.

"What's going on?" I asked, marching over to the closet. I looked inside. Mr. Foyle was gone. "What are the symptoms of a stroke?" I asked Spencer.

"So, you weren't hiding anything from me?" he asked, disappointed.

"No, you were right." I picked up one of the bowling ball bags and handed it to him. "Here. I got this for you. Happy birthday."

"You got me a pink bowling ball bag?"

"Look inside."

He unzipped it. "You got me a pink bowling ball in a pink bowling ball bag?"

"Surprise!"

I had broken out in a flop sweat, and I wiped my forehead with the back of my arm. If I had been thinking clearer, I would have handed him the bow and arrow set. But I was flipping out. Two dead men had somehow managed to escape. They could pop up anywhere.

"So, let's go," I said. "You found me out. I'm hungry."

"All right," he said, looking at his bowling ball.

I put on my coat and opened the front door. "Don't wait up," I told the sisters.

"Have a wonderful time," Sarah called.

Spencer followed me and closed the door behind us. "Where's your car?" I asked.

"Here," he said, pointing at a Porsche in the driveway.

"That's not your car. You have a sedan."

"That's my work car. This is my me car."

He opened the passenger door for me. "So, there's things I don't know about you, huh?"

"Like I'm a bowler."

"Are you a bowler?" I asked.

"No."

The steakhouse was fancier than I expected. A coat-check girl took our coats, and there was a woman playing a harp in the corner. Candles lit the tables, and the main room was awash in a glow from the fire in a large fireplace.

"It's so romantic," I said.

Spencer pulled me close and kissed my neck. "Good. It's part of my evil plan."

We were the only ones there, probably because it was only five o'clock. The maître d' welcomed us and took us to a center table. Spencer pulled my chair out for me, and I sat. The maître d' handed us menus, and a young man filled our glasses with water and put a basket of bread on the table. I grabbed some bread with one hand, and Spencer grabbed my other hand.

"Well," he said, locking eyes with me. He caressed my palm with his finger, making small circles. It was the most erotic thing I had ever felt, and he knew it. His lips turned up slightly, not in his normal smirk and not in a smile, but in something else, like he had discovered the secret to Gladie and he was going to take it to the bank. Boy, did I want him to take it to the bank. I was sure that that bank was chock full of orgasms and screams of ecstasy.

"Well," I repeated, dropping the bread.

"This is going to be very good." Spencer's voice dripped sex. The good kind of sex. The best kind of sex. He brought my hand to his mouth and kissed it. It lasted a long time, and when he finally gave me back my hand, I worried that I was pregnant.

Pregnant by hand kissing.

I was definitely going to use my grandmother's condoms tonight. All twelve of them.

"Are you going to answer that?" Spencer asked.

"What?"

"Your phone's ringing."

"It is?"

"Yes. Your *Night Fever* ringtone is playing."

I shook my head, clearing out the hormones. Spencer was right. My phone was ringing. I dug it out of my purse. It was Ruth. I answered.

"Hold on," I said into the phone. "I'm going to take this," I told Spencer.

"Do you want me to order for you?"

"Yes, anything steak and potato is good with me."

I walked back to the bathroom. "Ruth. Ruth," I said into the phone, my panic coming back. "You'll never guess what happened."

"What are you doing?" she demanded. "Are you investigating? Did you find anything out? Evidence? Clues?"

"Hold on, there. I'm out to dinner with Spencer. But I have something to tell you."

"You're on a date with the cop? What's the matter with you, girl? I know you must have a brain because you walk and talk, but you don't have a lick of common sense."

"Ruth. Ruth," I interrupted. "Ruth, I'm trying to tell you something. The bodies. Mr. Foyle and Mr. Tracy, they disappeared."

"They didn't disappear," Ruth said.

"They did. They're not there. Either they weren't really dead, or they got sucked up into the portal of hell."

"Oh for goodness sake. There's no portal of hell. They were really dead, and before you offer another explanation, there's no such thing as zombies."

"Zombies! I didn't think about zombies. That could be it. They're probably wandering around that house looking for brains."

"Well, then you don't have anything to worry about," Ruth growled. "Listen, Einstein. I moved the bodies."

"Excuse me?"

"I moved them."

"Where did you move them? Did you drive around town with two stiffs in my car? Don't tell me they're still in there."

"They're not in my car," she said. "Is it important where I moved them to?"

"Uh, let me think about that a minute. Yes!"

"Okay. Okay. I buried them in the snow in the back of the house by the shed. That way they won't stink."

"You put them on ice?" I asked.

"Genius, right?"

It was kind of genius, and now I wouldn't have to stay in a house with rotting corpses in it. Instead, they would be frozen solid in the snow below my bedroom window. It was a step in the right direction.

"I can't believe I'm in this position," I said. "How did I get in this position? Other people spend their entire lives never finding one murder victim. Not one. I trip over them on a regular basis, like they're Legos or something. Now, I'm hiding two in the snow. In the snow, Ruth. In the snow."

"Focus, would you? I'm old. I can't waste precious minutes listening to you babble all the time. So, get on the stick, would you? Find out who killed the old men. Remember, you won't get the car without it. Get out of there and start playing detective like you're supposed to."

"Ruth, nothing is going to cut my date short. Nothing. I'm seeing this through until the end. A nuclear bomb won't stop this date, do you hear me?"

But she didn't hear me. She had already hung up. I peed, and went back into the dining room. There were a few more diners, and a waitress was pouring wine into Spencer's glass. He stood when I entered. I sat down, and the waitress poured wine into my glass. "I'm Fionnula, and I'll be your server this evening," she said and then she recognized me, and I recognized her. It was Fionnula Jericho, the woman suing me for eight-hundred-thousand-dollars.

"You!" she shouted, dropping the wine bottle. "You!"

CHAPTER 11

A lot of matches, once they're matched, go zoom! Lightning fast. But others... Oy, gavalt. You could die from such indecision. They go on a date, they schmooze, they go on another date, they pull back. This way. That way. Round and round. You know what I mean? They investigate little by little. And you're the matchmaker, and you're thinking: Nu? Get on with it! But I have to tell you, bubeleh, love takes many forms. Some fast. Some slow. Sometimes, the slow ones are the real winners in the long run, just like the turtle and the bunny rabbit story. So, let your matches be turtles. Let them dip a toe in and investigate.

Lesson 117 Matchmaking Advice from Your Grandma Zelda

"You!" Fionnula screamed at me, again.

"You two know each other?" Spencer asked.

"Fionnula is a lovely woman, and I'm going to help her find a match. Free of charge," I said, smiling as wide as I could. It was a last-ditch effort to calm her down and hopefully change her mind about suing me. But from the look of her, no way was it going to work. In fact, it would be a miracle if I got out of the restaurant in one piece.

Why didn't I bring Lucy's cattle prod?

"Oh, I see. Another satisfied customer," Spencer said, sarcasm dripping from every word.

"You couldn't find a match if it lit your nose on fire," Fionnula screeched. "Did you know that I'm an award-winning Grand Theft Auto gamer? Did you know that?"

I had no idea, but I wasn't sure it was wise to tell her that.

"And I have a collection of antique paperclips." She picked up my salad fork and brandished it like a weapon. "I deserve love."

"Yes, you do," I said and braced for impact.

Spencer grabbed her wrist. "Drop it. Let's calm down, shall we?"

"I'm going to sue you for everything you're worth," she yelled.

"I buy socks on layaway," I said. "My insurance gave me $38.50 for my car when it blew up."

Fionnula yanked her hand out of Spencer's grip and took my wine glass. "You promised me love," she screeched and threw the contents of the glass into my face.

"Okay, that's it," Spencer said. He stood and picked up Fionnula by her waist with one arm, like she was a bag of dirty laundry. She kicked and swung her arms, knocking over glasses and dishes, as he carried her to the kitchen, where he dropped her off.

When he returned to the table, I was drying myself off with a napkin. "I guess we could go to Burger Boy," he said, as if someone had shot his dog.

"I could go for onion rings."

Spencer looked me up and down. "I guess I should have ordered the white wine instead of the red."

I was a mess. I had big splotches of red wine all over me. We left in a hurry before Fionnula could steal a meat cleaver and go after me in a serious way.

"This isn't going to put the kibosh on our date," Spencer said, shutting the car door behind me. Spencer walked around the car and sat in the driver's seat. "Nothing is going to stop this momentum."

He kissed me. It wasn't a normal, passion-filled Spencer kiss that threatened to make the top of my head blow off. This was a quiet, tender kiss that went on and on, like we had all the time in the world and our lips should always touch, tasting each other. Spencer touched my breast, the back of his fingers gliding over the underside and then over my nipple.

I was ready to get naked. The Porsche was small with a daunting stick shift, but at least the windows were tinted. Sure,

I would be more comfortable doing the dirty deed with Spencer in his bed, but by the time we got to his place, my ovaries would explode from the surge in estrogen production brought on from the kiss and his magical fingers caressing my breast.

Then, Foreigner starting singing "Jukebox Hero," and Spencer stopped kissing me. He punched his steering wheel.

"Sonofabitch!" he complained. "I can't catch a break."

"What's happening?" I asked in a fog of take-me-now.

He took his phone out of his pocket, and Foreigner stopped singing. "What!" He listened for a minute. "Are you kidding me? What the hell kind of town is this?" He turned off the phone and started the car.

"I have to take you home," he said between clenched teeth.

"What happened?" I asked and crossed my fingers that Mr. Foyle and Mr. Tracy hadn't been found in the backyard.

"Crazy townspeople are fighting about who the founder was. Can you believe it? They're throwing things at each other in Cannes Center Park. You know, I moved here for a little peace and quiet. You know, hiking in the mountains. That sort of thing."

"You hike?"

"No."

I woke up at six-thirty from the smell of fresh bread baking downstairs. The sun was rising, and the house seemed warm and cozy. It was a stark difference from the night before. Spencer had driven me home, driving like a maniac, pushing his sports car to the limits. His phone rang twice more during the drive, provoking a whole slew of swearing from him. By the time he dropped me off at Ruth's sisters' house, he was so distracted that he didn't kiss me goodnight, and he didn't offer any promises to see me later.

When Naomi opened the front door for me, she was understandably surprised. "Holy moly, he's fast. A quickie, huh?"

"No quickie. Our dinner was cut short because he had to work."

Naomi and Sarah invited me to eat dinner with them. I ate homemade chicken pot pie, salad, and homemade ice cream for dessert. It was definitely a step up from eating takeout with my grandmother. My fears of them being psychotic killers faded into the background with each delicious bite. I went to bed early with a borrowed book, and it wasn't until after I got into bed that I was overcome with the spookiness of the home.

Again, I wondered if there were other dead men in the house, if Naomi and Sarah were killers, and if there really was a portal to hell. I locked my bedroom door and wedged a chair under the doorknob just to be on the safe side.

But after some initial struggle, I slept soundly. With the smell of fresh baked bread in my nose, I got out of bed in the morning and stretched by the window. Outside, the sun was shining without a cloud in the sky. I opened the window, expecting a rush of cold air, but the weather had changed, and it wasn't cold. We had been having a record-breaking winter, and I wonder if it was over, or if this was just a temporary break in weather.

After dressing in jeans, a sweater, and boots, I went downstairs and ate breakfast with the sisters. Homemade bread, butter, and jam, with delicious coffee instead of their regular tea. Lucy arrived thirty minutes early.

She was wearing tailored tweed pants, a silk blouse, and high heels. "Ruth, is that you?" Naomi asked, answering the door. Lucy breezed by her. "Darlin', there isn't one inch of me that could be confused with Ruth. My, isn't this lovely. I always wondered who lived in this house."

I introduced her and gathered my coat. Lucy put her hand over her mouth. "Do they know about the you know what?" she whispered to me.

"I'll tell you in the car," I said, putting on my coat.

The doorbell rang, and Naomi trotted to the door. "I love company," she gushed. Opening the door, she was greeted by an old man.

"Hello there, Miss Fletcher, how are you today?"

"Look, Sarah, Mr. Judd is here."

He entered the house. Mr. Judd was about the same age as Mr. Foyle and Mr. Tracy. He had a gorgeous head of thick, white hair. He was trim, dressed in khakis and a polo shirt, and he was only about five-foot-three, a couple inches shorter than Ruth's sisters.

"Nice to have met you all," Lucy said, walking toward the door, but I was frozen in place. I was trying to decide what to do. Sarah left the room to get Mr. Judd tea and bread, and I was wondering if he was victim number three.

I tried to catch Naomi's eye, but she was busy with Mr. Judd. At least, she sat him on the couch instead of the chair, but I was worried.

"Are we leaving?" Lucy asked.

"Uh…"

"I've always loved the woodworking in this house," Mr. Judd told Naomi. "Maybe later, I can look around some more, get some ideas for my place?"

Oh my God. Mr. Judd was a goner. I wondered what piece of furniture they would stuff him into.

"Gladie?" Lucy asked.

"Just a second."

I ran into the kitchen. Sarah was setting up the tea cart. "Sarah, don't kill Mr. Judd," I urged her.

"What?"

"Mr. Judd. I have to leave now, and I don't want him to wind up dead before I get back."

"Don't worry, Gladie. We'll protect him from the portal of hell."

I guessed that was as good of an assurance as I was going to get. I thought about kicking Mr. Judd out of the house, but he seemed pleased as punch to be visiting. Ruth's sisters were like catnip to elderly men. I made a note to figure out their secret to attraction, later, for professional reasons.

I walked back into the parlor. Mr. Judd was still alive. He was talking to Naomi on the couch. "Well, we're going," I told them. "Hey, Mr. Judd, you want to come with us? We can give you a ride."

"Thank you, but I came in my own car. I'm just going to hang around here for a couple hours before I head over to the high school. I tutor there a couple times a week. I'm a retired American history teacher."

He was a nice guy. I hated to think he would never make it to his tutoring. "Okay, well, we're going now," I said. "Leaving, but I'll be back soon. Or not. What I mean is, you'll never know when I might show up. To, I mean, witness. Yes, witness. So, I'm leaving, now. Okay…"

"What the devil are you talking about?" Lucy asked me.

"Just saying goodbye."

I gave Mr. Judd one last look before Lucy and I left the house. Outside, it was already about seventy degrees. "It's whiplash weather," I said. "One day freezing blizzards and the next day sun and seventy degrees."

"It's supposed to get up to eighty today," Lucy said, unlocking her Mercedes with a beep. We got in the car, and she started it. "Where to?"

I told her about the two dead men and how they were hidden and how I was tasked to solve the mystery before the day after tomorrow, and that I was going to get Ruth's car.

"Holy Garth Brooks," Lucy said. "You're a professional detective now. You've got your first real case. This is so good. I wonder if you'll be on the news."

I reminded her that we had to keep it secret for a couple

of days or until I solved the mystery or there would be no car for me and certain jail for Sarah and Naomi. "They can torture me, but I won't talk," Lucy promised.

I gave her a slip of paper that the sisters had given me with Mr. Foyle's address on it. The house wasn't far away. Lucy drove down the road and turned left on Serenity Village's main street of fancy tract houses.

The nice weather brought out the neighbors. The street had a steady stream of golf carts and speed-walkers on the sidewalks. Dwight Foyle lived in a ranch style house, but there was a granny flat built onto his garage.

Lucy parked two doors down on the street so we wouldn't attract attention. We walked to Mr. Foyle's house, looking both ways before we ducked in the bushes by the front window and peeked in. Inside, there was no sign of activity. No one was home.

"Let's try the door," I said.

We climbed out of the bushes and tried the door, but it was locked. "Don't worry," Lucy said. "I made some special purchases just for this occasion."

She took a small leather pouch out of her purse. She opened it and took out three, small metal tools. "Lock picks," she explained. "Here. Pick the lock."

She handed them to me. "Lucy, I have no idea how to

pick a lock."

"It can't be that hard. Haven't you ever watched Magnum P.I.?"

"I've watched it, but I was distracted by Tom Selleck's chest hair."

Lucy stuck her finger in the leather pouch and came out with a small piece of paper. "Here are the instructions," she said. "Let's see. Okay. I think I got it. First you stick the bendy one in the key hole," she said. I did as she instructed. "Now, take the curvier, bendy one and turn it."

"What about the third one? The straight one?"

"I think that one's extra."

"This is never going to work," I complained. "We should try for an open window."

"Oh, darn it. It looks so easy when Magnum does it."

I didn't want to disappoint her, especially since this was my first official case, and she was my back up. "Okay. I'll try."

I stuck the curvy, bendy tool in and turned, and like a miracle from the heavens, it worked the first time. I felt the lock turn, and I removed the lock picks. "I think it's done," I said.

Lucy turned the knob, and sure enough, the door opened. We looked to see if the coast was clear, and once a golf cart passed, we went inside.

Mr. Foyle was tidy. There was nothing on the floor and no dirty dishes in the sink. "I wish Uncle Harry was like this," Lucy said. "Harry needs a vacuum to follow him wherever he goes."

"Mr. Foyle was working on a big story. That's our best bet for a motive. Let's find his office."

His office was in the guest room. He had a small desk in the corner of the room. It was as tidy as the rest of his house. There was a place for unopened bills on top of the desk, and a drawer of files for the paid bills. It didn't look like he was working on any kind of story. Then, we found a memo pad.

"Eureka,' Lucy said.

I tried to read it. "It's gibberish. I can't make out anything."

"It's shorthand."

"Can you read it?"

"No," Lucy said. "But Harry's secretary can. Should I take it to him?"

It was stealing, but since we were already hiding dead bodies and breaking and entering, I didn't see how stealing a memo pad could make things worse. "Sure. Good idea."

She slipped the pad into her purse. "Where now?"

"Mr. Tracy's house, I guess."

There was a loud noise above our heads, like something had hit the floor. Or someone. Then we heard a door slam, and footsteps walking down from the granny flat. Lucy and I clutched each other in a hug.

"We've been found out," she whispered.

"Did you bring your cattle prod?"

"You told me no weapons."

I looked around for a weapon, but aside from a pen, I couldn't find anything. As the voices came closer, I could make out what they were saying.

"Lenny, the old man doesn't eat chips. He eats old school, like meatloaf and shit," one of the voices said.

"Meatloaf sounds good, too," the other voice said. "You think it goes with onion dip?"

"They don't sound dangerous," I whispered to Lucy. "We should probably make ourselves known."

Holding on to each other, we tiptoed out of the guest room. In the kitchen, two young men were riffling through the cabinets and the refrigerator, looking for snacks. The one with the beard had found a canister of fried onions, and the one with long hair had his head in the fridge.

"Hello," I said, softly. The one with the beard stepped back in surprise. "We come in peace," I assured him.

"Unless you mess with us and then I'll karate chop your balls," Lucy added.

"Are you Dwight's friends?" the long haired one asked.

"Uh," I said.

"I'm Lenny, and this is Moe. We rent the apartment upstairs."

They reeked of pot. I was getting a contact high off the fumes from their clothes, which were board shorts and muscle-T's. Ironic wear, since they were blindingly white like they had never seen sun, and they had zero muscle tone.

"Haven't we met?" Lucy asked Lenny.

"I don't know, man. I'm a postdoctoral student, working on my thesis on ethics."

So, the pothead had forty more IQ points than I did. "Lenny, you wouldn't know what story Dwight was working on, do you?" I asked.

"Story?" Moe asked. "Oh, RIP. I told you he was really Stephen King. That's off the charts, man."

"He's not like Stephen King," Lenny told him. "Moe's like a horror fan," Lenny explained to us.

"He's not Stephen King," I repeated.

Moe slapped his forehead. "Damn. Yeah, that's right. Dwight's got a few years on Stephen King. That would have been cool, though. Sometimes things get foggy in my brain."

"It's all that weed," Lucy said.

"Weed's like my medicine, man," Moe said. "But I used to take drugs. Heroin. Bad stuff. Don't use, man. It messes with you."

I gave Lenny my number and asked him to call me if he remembered anything about Mr. Foyle's story, after explaining that he was a journalist, not a novelist. Lenny and Moe didn't ask us anything about Mr. Foyle's whereabouts or why we were in the house. We left them to ransack the kitchen and walked back to Lucy's car.

The phone rang. It was Ruth. "Where are you?" she demanded.

"I'm working on the case, like you told me to."

"Well, forget it. Get back here. I need your help."

"Where?" I asked. "What do you want? I'm busy."

"At my sisters' house, of course. Haven't you noticed

the weather?"

I put my hand over the phone. "Sorry, Lucy," I said. "She's such a pain in the ass. She's going on about the weather."

"I can hear you," Ruth said in the phone. "Listen, genius. It's hot outside. Hot. You know what that means?"

"That I don't have to wear a coat."

"And the snow is melting. Melting," she said, dragging out the last word.

"Oh my God."

"Get over here, quick. I can already see an arm. It's only a matter of minutes before the neighborhood is going to get an eyeful of dead people. And I can't move them on my own. My sisters went to a quilting meeting or wherever they go."

"I'll be right over."

CHAPTER 12

Dolly, sometimes no good deed goes unpunished. I don't mean to toot my own horn, but toot, toot, toot. I've done a lot of good deeds. But sometimes the good-for-nothing putzes of this world take my good deeds and turn them on their head and say: Hey, you! You did a bad deed, and I'm mad at you, like they're a good deed maven and not the stupid putz that they are. This is a no-good part of being in the love business. I don't do well with mad. I only know love. So, I use that love like a weapon. I shoot it back at those putzes who are mad at me. Sometimes it doesn't work, but other times, it works like a dream. You see, love is contagious. Just like the flu.

Lesson 40, Matchmaking Advice from Your
Grandma Zelda

Lucy dropped me off at Ruth's sisters' house, and she went to get to the memo pad translated. Ruth's car was parked in the driveway. Once again, I wondered if it was worth all of this trouble.

The front door opened, and Ruth stepped out. "Hurry up," she urged. She was wearing an apron and Platex gloves, and her face was glistening with sweat.

"I'm here."

"Hustle your butt, girl. This is serious business."

I didn't want to enter the house. I didn't want to do whatever it was that Ruth wanted me to do that required an apron and Platex gloves.

Ruth put her gloved hands on her hips. "Come on, you're not going to abandon an old lady in her time of need."

"Well…"

Ruth grabbed my left ear and yanked hard, forcing me to walk into the house. I slapped her hand away and rubbed my ear. "Geez, Ruth. That hurt." I stopped speaking and froze in place with my arms out to my sides, like they would help me catch my balance. "Holy shitballs. What happened to the chair?"

The portal to hell chair was still in its place, but the upholstery had been slashed three ways to Sunday. "Poor Mr. Judd," I breathed. "They got him."

Ruth grabbed my shoulders in a death grip and got in my face. "Listen, Gladie. This shit's getting real. Do you understand me?"

I shook my head. Of course, I didn't understand her. I had left about an hour before and everything was fine. Mr. Judd was about to eat bread and drink tea.

"Listen, girl," she continued, her eyes wild, like a steer

about to be butchered. "I lied about Sarah and Naomi. I have no idea where they are. They disappeared."

"Into the portal of hell?"

Ruth pinched me hard. I slapped her hands away and backed up out of her range. "Ruth, you're a pacifist. Stop hurting me."

She took a deep breath. "I'm sorry. I'm sorry. Okay. I'm calm now."

Ruth didn't look calm. She had passed one of her Platex gloves over her head, making her hair stand up on end. She was sweating for real, now. "There's no portal of hell, Gladie. There's two dead men melting outside, and my sisters are missing."

"What about Mr. Judd?"

"Who?"

"He was here when I left. An old guy, like the rest."

As if we were reading each other's minds, we high-tailed it to the window seat. It was empty, just like the night before. We ran to the closet under the stairs. No corpses.

"Where else could they have hidden them?" I asked.

"We don't have time for that right now. We have to hide the bodies before they're found out."

"Ruth, I think it's time to bring in the cops."

She shook her finger at me. "You promised me. You gave me three days. How's your investigation?"

"I broke into Mr. Foyle's house and got a memo pad of his notes," I explained. "It's being translated now because it was in shorthand. And he has two junkies living above his garage who are going to contact me if they think of anything. So, I don't have much, yet."

"That's fine," Ruth said. "I know you can do it. It's just two more days. What's two more days going to do?"

Sometimes a person goes crazy, and you just have to let them live in Crazy Town for a while. No amount of logic can bring them around. So, I didn't point out that her sisters were probably the murderers, and if they weren't, their lives might be in danger, now that they were missing. No, I just let Ruth roll around in her crazy-mobile, spouting her crazy language, and did as I was told. Maybe she was right. Maybe her sisters were quilting and were perfectly innocent, and maybe I would find the real culprit within forty-eight hours, and all of this would be just a bad memory.

Ruth opened the back door. The snow had melted incredibly fast. Poor Mr. Foyle and Mr. Tracy. They were half melted, still rolled into balls. "You know, if this wasn't so disgusting and wrong, this would be kind of funny," I said.

"Keep it together, girl."

"What's your plan, Ruth?"

"We're going to bring them in and stuff them into the freezers in the cellar. I've already cleared them out."

"When you say, 'we're going to bring them in,' what do you mean by that?" I asked.

"We're going to do what I did before with my sisters. We're going to heave ho them onto the tea carts, push them back into the house, pushed them down the stairs, tea cart them again, and dump them into the freezers."

I slapped my hand over my mouth. "Ruth, I ate off those tea carts."

She didn't care. It was time to get down to business. I took off my clothes, down to my underpants, bra, and boots so that my clothes wouldn't get dead people cooties on them. Ruth gave me another apron and a pair of Platex gloves, and I tied a tea towel around my head, like a mask.

I still had a fifty percent chance of passing out. I had spent a lifetime being squeamish, but after the past five months, I had had a lot of experience with dead people.

Ruth and I took a tea cart each and rolled them through the house, through the back door to the outside. Ruth parked her cart by Mr. Foyle. She crouched down and grabbed legs, leaving me his other half. It took us three tries to lift him, but we finally loaded him onto the tea cart.

Mr. Tracy was another story. He had about fifty pounds on Mr. Foyle, and we were already tired. "I've got an idea," Ruth said. She went to the shed and came back with a plank of wood. We wedged one end under Mr. Tracy and rested the other end on my tea cart. "We'll roll him."

Rolling him turned out to be very difficult. I crouched down and tucked my hands under him, pushing until my arms were under Mr. Tracy up to my elbows. "Gross. Gross. Gross," I repeated like a mantra. For some reason, complaining helped battle the nausea, and I didn't throw up once. Ruth pulled from up above, while I pushed up. We repeated the process four times, and it took at least fifteen minutes to finally get him on my tea cart that way. By the time we had both bodies on the tea carts, we were so exhausted that we collapsed onto the rest of the snow and tried to catch our breath for a minute.

"Don't you dare drop dead, Ruth," I said, my heart pounding. "I don't want to deal with you, too."

She panted and wheezed. "I'll never complain about a breathing human, again. I've had my fill of death."

"Ditto."

"We have to work quickly," Ruth said. "The old folks like to take walks in these woods. It's just a matter of time

elise sax

before we're found out."

I stood and adjusted the towel around my face. Offering Ruth my hand, I pulled her up. She began to push her tea cart, and I pushed mine. Rolling over the pavement wasn't difficult, but it was slow going, keeping one hand on Mr. Tracy to prevent him from falling off. Getting over the door's threshold was a different matter, and it took both of us to get each tea cart into the house.

Ruth closed the door behind us. I retied my apron, which had gotten loose. I was happy to be half-naked because moving two bodies was a strenuous workout, and the temperature was rising. Meanwhile, Ruth was still in her turtleneck, which was drenched through with sweat. She parked her tea cart at a door on the other side of the staircase, and I parked mine behind hers. After she opened the door, I took a peek.

"The cellar," she explained. "All the canning and jarring is done down there."

"Do you hear that?" I asked. There was a faint bell sound.

"It's not the doorbell."

"It's not my phone."

And it wasn't the dead men's phones. It was a soft sound, like an old-fashioned bell, but it was getting louder.

FROM FEAR TO ETERNITY

"Who's cares?" Ruth said. "I need to finish with this. I left Tea Time in Julie's hands, and I need to get back to it. She probably burned it down by now. And my back's killing me. And my knees. And the arthritis in my hands. And my neck."

"I get it. All right. So, what are we doing?"

"Simple. We're going to tip the cart over and let him slide off and fall down the stairs."

"That's pretty cold," I said.

"Hey, there's no crying in body moving."

Three things happened simultaneously. First, I wondered, again, why I was doing this. Second, Ruth and I lifted one half of the tea cart up, grunting loudly, but Mr. Foyle didn't budge. And third and probably most importantly, Spencer Bolton—my boyfriend and Chief of Police—opened the front door, bringing in a brand new, pink bicycle with a basket and bell, which he was ringing repeatedly until he noticed Ruth and me, our two tea carts, and the two dead men on them.

Then, he stopped ringing the bell.

Spencer's mouth dropped open, but he didn't say a word. The bike slipped from his hands and dropped sideways onto the parlor floor.

"It's not what it looks like," Ruth said. Mr. Foyle chose

that moment to slip free of the tea cart. He landed with a terrifying sound onto the stairs and just like Ruth said would happen, he fell, plop, plop, plop, down the stairs and came to a stop on the cellar floor.

"What?" Spencer bellowed. "What? What? What?"

I took the towel off my face and removed my gloves and the apron. Spencer stared at me in my underwear and boots. "What?" he said.

"It's kind of a long story," I said and took a seat on the couch. It was good to sit down. Accessory after the fact was exhausting.

Ruth was looking at Mr. Tracy, and for a moment I thought she was weighing her options. But it was obvious that there weren't options. The jig was up. Our goose was cooked. The fat lady sang. Elvis left the building. In other words, we were shit out of luck.

Ruth took off her gloves and threw them down on the tea cart in defeat. She walked to the sofa and plopped down next to me. Spencer inspected Mr. Tracy for a moment and then sat down on the portal to hell.

"You probably shouldn't sit there," I told him.

"Why not?"

"Well, it's possible that two or three men were killed

there, and some say it's the portal to hell. Is that bike for me?"

Spencer ran his fingers through his hair. "I was being romantic, trying to make up for cutting our date short last night."

"That's really sweet." I didn't often get gifts, especially not thoughtful ones.

"It's not as good as a pink bowling ball, but…"

"How long is this torture going to last?" Ruth complained. "Dates, romance, bikes. What the hell? It's like a cat playing with a mouse before it eats it. Just bring out the handcuffs and get on with it."

"Okay," Spencer said. "What charges? What are we talking about? Murder? Torture? Kidnapping?"

"Oh, phew. We didn't do any of those. Isn't that a relief, Ruth?" I asked. "So, can we just call this a wash? No harm, no foul? Just one of those things? A simple indiscretion? No harm done? Happy ending? No hard feelings? No hassle? No hang-ups? Oh, please stop me. My mouth won't stop."

"So, what did you do?" asked Spencer. He was very calm, under the circumstances. Usually, he scolded me when I got in trouble. But now he was emotionless. He wasn't even blinking.

"It's kind of funny, actually," I said, smiling wide. "I'm

sure you'll laugh."

"I like to laugh. So tell me."

I shivered. "Remember, we're in a relationship."

He smiled, slightly. It wasn't a Spencer smile. It was a chief of police smile. I tried to swallow but my throat was constricted with panic.

"I'll tell you everything," Ruth said. And she did. She told him about finding the bodies and twisting my arm to investigate the deaths. She told him about the snow and the tea carts. Spencer was quiet for a long time after and then called the coroner and Remington Cumberbatch, his detective and my ex-casual sex partner.

"You two should get changed, or dressed in your case, Gladie," Spencer said after Ruth's explanation.

Ruth and I walked upstairs, while Spencer stood guard downstairs. "Look at what you did," Ruth hissed at me, as we climbed the stairs.

"Oh, wow. You're not putting this on me. You're the one moving around bodies. You're the one who wanted to hide what your sisters did."

"My sisters are innocent. If you weren't flashing your hoo-ha to every male in town, the chief of police wouldn't have walked in before we could freeze the stiffs."

"Do you hear yourself?" I demanded. "Freeze the stiffs?"

"Now my sisters are going to spend the rest of their years in lockup. That's on you," she said, jabbing my chest with her finger.

We arrived at the second floor. "It's on me?" I asked.

"That's on you," she said, punctuating each word by poking my chest. "You should have found the real murderers, and you shouldn't have brought the cop around."

She was right. It was on me. But I didn't want to be responsible for two old ladies rotting away in prison. I walked up to the third floor to my bedroom with guilt weighing heavily on me. I was also worried about my relationship with Spencer. For the first time since I had met him, he had been cold to me. Usually, he was either hot and heavy with me or irritated and impatient with me. Never cold.

I walked into my bedroom, slipped on sweats and a t-shirt, and sat on the bed. My eyes filled with tears. I had screwed up everything. Miss Marple would have never gotten into this mess. She would have solved the mystery within fifteen minutes. She would have been able to read shorthand, and she would never have moved dead bodies.

I heard footsteps in the hallway, and I figured that Ruth had come back to yell at me some more, but it was worse. Spencer walked into my room and closed the door behind him.

"Are you kidding me?" he said. "Can't you keep out of trouble for five minutes? For once in your life? You're a trouble magnet. You're a jinx." Spencer paced the room, swinging his arms wildly. "There I was, bringing you a bike. With a bell, Pinky! A bell!"

"I like bells," I said, wiping my nose on my hand.

"And there you were. You know. With two dead men. Not one. Two. Two! One on a cart, and the other you dumped down the stairs." He pointed to the floor. "Down the stairs! You threw a dead guy down the stairs!"

"Not exactly threw. You see, we tipped the cart, and he slipped off."

Spencer put his finger up to his mouth. "Shh. Don't say anything. It raises my blood pressure, and I've already reached stroke-level. Where was I? I was saying something. Oh, yeah, now I remember. Only you! Only you find dead bodies in furniture." He took my hand. "Come on."

"Where are we going?"

"To the station."

I sniffed. "The police station? Am I going to jail?"

"It would be safer for the world if you did go to jail. But I just need you to give your official statement."

Downstairs, it was all hands on deck, inspecting the house. Mr. Foyle was zipped into a body bag, and Mr. Tracy was being hauled up from the cellar. Outside, Spencer put Ruth and me in the back of his sedan. We passed Bird's salon on the way to the station. "Closed due to intergalactic war," was written on a handmade sign on the door. A little further, Fred, in his pest control uniform, ran out of the pharmacy with his spray can, spraying behind him in a panic.

"Poor Fred," I said.

"Good riddance," Spencer said. "I've got a lead on a great desk sergeant in San Diego. I'm going to offer him a job after this mess is taken care of."

I figured I was "this mess." "Fred thinks he's a screw-up. You need to tell him to come back. He's scared of bugs."

"He thinks he's a screw-up because he is a screw-up," Spencer said.

"I'll second that," Ruth said. "But the boy is miserable, and sometimes people deserve a second chance. Life's hard enough without forgiveness."

It was pretty deep for Ruth, a real step up from her usual tirades.

At the station, Spencer separated us, took our official statements, and then let us go. "Don't get into more trouble, Gladys," he told me in his office, pulling me close. "I don't want to see you hurt. I've gotten kind of used to you."

"Don't call me Gladys."

"Don't hide dead people. It's going to take some acrobats on my part to keep you out of this mess. They're sending the bodies over to San Diego for the autopsies, and I've ordered a rush. A buddy is going to move them to the front of the line. Hopefully, it will turn out to be natural causes, and I can keep Ruth's sisters out of the slammer."

I had my doubts about keeping Ruth's sisters out of the slammer, but I decided to keep my mouth shut.

"So, do we have a deal? You let me do the investigating?" he asked, nuzzling my ear.

"Believe me, nothing could make me get involved again. I've had enough of dead old men."

Outside, it was good to breathe the air as a free woman. Ruth was waiting for me and pulled me aside. "The deal's still on," she told me. "While they're investigating, you're going to keep investigating."

"But Spencer told me to keep out of trouble."

"What trouble? You're investigating, not robbing a bank. Come on, Gladie, help my sisters. And don't forget the car. You owe me."

I was pretty sure a car wasn't worth me getting into more trouble. I was about to tell her that I was done with the whole mess when her breathing hitched, and tears ran down her face. It was the first time I had ever seen Ruth cry. In fact, I had been reasonably sure that she didn't possess tear ducts.

The burst of emotion made me emotional, too. For all of Ruth complaining about her sisters, she was worried about them. I was an only child, and I could only imagine the bond of siblings.

"Sure, Ruth, I'll do it. I won't let you down."

She wiped her tears and sniffed. "You better not let me down," she growled and walked away without turning back.

What had I gotten myself into?

CHAPTER 13

The plot thickens. Isn't that what they say? Matches start off with a little bit of willingness. Sometimes chemistry. But then it builds. If it doesn't build, pull your match back and assure him or her that another match is around the corner. That's your job. You're like the referee of love. But if you see a spark in the match, then let it build. Let the plot get really thick. Keep them in the game.

Lesson 110, Matchmaking Advice from Your Grandma Zelda

Standing outside the police station, I wondered how I would get home and where my home was. I couldn't go to my actual home because it was being tented for bed bugs. Even though I was supposed to be investigating two deaths in Ruth's sisters' house, I didn't want to go back there. Wherever I was going to stay, I didn't have a way to get there. I took out my phone and began to call Bridget, when Lucy's Mercedes screeched to a stop at the curb.

Lucy opened the passenger window. "Get in," she said. "I can't believe I missed it," she complained when I took a seat and put on my seatbelt. "All the excitement happens when I'm gone."

Wow, news sure traveled fast in our town. "What did you hear?"

"Well, I heard several renditions. I heard that you were

a necrophiliac in a necrophilia club, which was raided."

"Oh, yuck."

"I also heard that you were creating a Frankenstein monster," she said. I nodded. That was closer to the truth. "But Betsy Langston at the Chevron said you had murdered two old men and Spencer caught you while you were burying them in the cellar. I tend to believe her because she's got a scanner and lives real close to the power lines."

"It's kind of the truth if you squint your eyes," I said.

"The minute I heard you had been arrested, I rushed over here," Lucy explained, excited. "I think I ran over a possum, but I didn't stop to see."

"Thank you, but I wasn't arrested. Just questioned."

"I bet you were, darlin'. I have loads of questions for you, too. What happened? Where are the dead guys? Who done it?"

I explained the whole debacle to Lucy. "He bought you a bicycle?" she asked.

"That's the part of the story that caught your attention?"

"Well, it's sort of a weird gift."

"It wasn't the Hope Diamond," I agreed. "But it was

thoughtful. Yesterday, I was riding a bike, and I got hit by a bus and then the bike was stolen. See?"

"Lord have mercy. I miss everything."

"I wish I missed everything," I said. "Where are we going?"

"Next stop, Ross Tracy. He was richer than Midas. Did you know that?"

I nodded. "I heard something about Roosevelt."

"Well, I bet a whole passel of people wanted him dead. Rich people attract haters like honey attracts flies. You still got the lock picks?"

Mr. Tracy's house was the same model as Mr. Foyle's but without the granny flat over the garage. It was on another street, a sort of wheel spoke to the wheel of small shops that served the community. It was old people paradise, just as clean as Disneyland but without the lines and theme music.

"I hear that Jack Palance lives here," Lucy said.

"Jack Palance is dead."

"Did I say Jack Palance? I meant Walter Matthau."

"He's dead, too." I was a high school dropout, but I knew my celebrity trivia.

"Holy Gone with Wind, do you think this place killed them?" Lucy asked. "Like maybe it's cursed? Like it kills men out of spite?"

It was as good of a theory as anything else, but I thought it had more to do with age, and I doubted Jack Palance or Walter Matthau ever lived in Apple Serenity Village.

Lucy parked the car in front of the Village Tavern, and we walked the half a block to Mr. Tracy's house.

"Gorgeous day," Lucy said. It was about eighty-five degrees and there wasn't a cloud in the sky. It was summer in January. A weird, mutant day that was a welcome relief from our harsh winter.

"Perfect day for more breaking and entering," I said. We stared at Mr. Tracy's front door. It was a turning point kind of moment. Spencer had just warned me not to get into more trouble, and here I was, digging in my purse for my lock picks. If I had more sense, I would have just gotten my free latte from Ruth and went home with Bridget to her nice, safe townhouse.

But I didn't think it was a matter of sense. It was more like I was an alcoholic, compulsively sucking down a box of wine without thinking. That was me. But in my case, I was a mystery-holic, compulsively snooping, even though it could

elise sax

wind me up in jail, or even worse, squash any chance I ever had of feeling Spencer's tongue on my how-do-you-do.

I stuck the lock picks into the lock, and just like the last time, it opened on my first try. "You're better than Magnum," Lucy said, impressed. "You could be in the CIA."

I pushed the door open halfway, but someone from inside pulled it open the rest of the way. It was a tiny woman, wearing scrubs. Her hair was pulled back, and she was holding a Swiffer with an extra-long handle.

"Maybe I help you?" she asked.

"Uh," I said.

"We're here to inspect the house," Lucy explained.

"That's actually true," I said, surprised.

"Inspect the house? Why?" the small lady asked.

"Did you know that Walter Matthau is dead?" I said and walked inside. Lucy followed, quickly.

The small woman wasn't alone. There was an entire cleaning team, working. "We won't be long," Lucy said, pushing me through the living room toward the bedrooms. Mr. Tracy's office was in the same place as Mr. Foyle's. His desk wasn't quite as organized, and it was bigger—a behemoth—with a large leather desk set on top and fancy gold pens.

Lucy rummaged through the drawers, and I sat in the chair and went through his calendar. According to it, he had a massage and shvitz every Friday and every Sunday met with Dwight, Ben, and Leslie for something.

"Who are they?" Lucy asked, leaning over my shoulder.

"Dwight must be Mr. Foyle, but I have no idea who Ben and Leslie are. What did you find? Any luck?"

Lucy held up a big silver ball with a plaque on it. "He won an award from General Motors for his service. I'm guessing not for pumping gas."

There was no clue about why he would have been murdered. "Maybe he just ate a lot of bacon," I said, hopefully.

"Or prostate cancer. That's an epidemic in this country."

I thought about Mr. Tracy's prostate for a minute, but we were interrupted by the roar of a vacuum approaching. I closed the calendar, and we walked out.

"I'll tell you something, Gladie. Timing is everything, and mine is terrible. I totally missed burying the dead bodies in the cellar, but am here for the desk search. My life is boring."

"We didn't bury the bodies in the cellar," I explained. "We just threw Mr. Foyle down the stairs. How about I make it up to you by letting you buy me lunch?"

We decided to try out the Village Tavern because we were parked in front of it, and they had a sandwich board outside, promising bottomless fries. The inside was a dead ringer for every English pub I had ever seen in the movies. There were about ten wood tables and chairs, and sawdust on the floor. The bar was massive, and the bartender was a large man with a handlebar mustache. The tavern was very busy, and its clientele was almost entirely male. Lucy and I took a seat by a wall. A waiter appeared quickly and suggested the fish and chips.

"Sounds good," I said.

"Do you have a Cobb salad?" Lucy asked.

"We have coleslaw," he said.

"Fine. I'll take the fish and chips."

"What's happening back there?" she asked and pointed to a back door, which men were walking in and out of.

"A wake for Dwight and Ross," the waiter explained. "We host a lot of those. People drop like flies around here. You're free to take part. It'll last all day until we close at ten."

The waiter left, and I clapped my hand on Lucy's arm. "You know what this means?" I asked.

"Yes. It's going to take four Zumba classes for me to work off this meal. I've got to wear a fitted mermaid wedding dress in a few weeks, you know."

"No. I mean, do you know what this means?" I said, pointing at the back door. "Reconnaissance. Intelligence. There's probably a dozen drunk suspects and witnesses here, who can give us the scoop."

Lucy's eyes grew wide and round like saucers. "The scoop. Oh, this is going to be good."

The waiter came back five minutes later with our fish and chips. I doused my food in ketchup, and it was delicious. The tavern filled up to the rafters while we ate. It seemed like every male octogenarian in Southern California was there.

That's when I spotted him.

"Oh, my God. He's alive," I said.

Lucy looked around, like a dog sniffing for leftover chicken. "Where? Who?"

"Mr. Judd. He came by Ruth's sister's house this morning, remember? But then he disappeared along with Sarah and Naomi. I was sure he was a goner."

He wasn't a goner. He looked pleased as punch. Getting a beer at the bar that he could barely see over, he was talking to a handful of other men who he seemed to know. I got up and practically ran to him.

"Mr. Judd, there you are. How are you?" I searched him for obvious signs of damage or attempted murder, but he looked just like he had looked earlier. Short, dapper, with a head of thick, white hair.

"Excuse me?" he asked.

"It's me. We met this morning, remember? You were visiting Sarah and Naomi."

"Oh, sure. Please call me Leslie."

Lucy and I exchanged looks. He was the Leslie on Mr. Tracy's calendar and met with the two victims once a week.

"So, Leslie, you're here for the wake?" Lucy asked. "You were friends with the deceased?"

"Yes, ever since I moved here three years ago. I'm a retired American history teacher." His eyes twinkled at Lucy, and his eyebrows did a little dance, like the retired American history teacher bit was his best pickup line with the ladies and it never failed. Lucy ran with it, slipping her arm through his.

"Tell me all about it," she purred.

With Leslie Judd being subtly questioned by a capable interrogator, I went out back to mix and mingle. The door led to a large courtyard. About thirty people sat at tables, and more were standing with drinks in their hands, getting sloshed and talking about sports, the fall of Western civilization, and Mr. Foyle and Mr. Tracy's demise.

I was a terrible mixer and mingler, in general. At my grandmother's parties, I usually found a bowl of peanuts and stayed with it, stuffing my face so I didn't have to talk with anyone. What was appropriate conversation with perfect strangers who were fifty years older than I was?

"Hello, girlie," a man in Bermuda shorts and a purple Izod shirt greeted me with a wide smile. "Are you Ross's granddaughter? You look just like him."

Ross Tracy was an eighty-something, extremely rotund man. "No," I said. "Friend of the family. I'm Cary Grant's granddaughter."

The man cocked his head to the side, trying to fit Cary Grant's face onto my head. "Were you friends with the deceased?" I asked.

"Oh, sure. Oh, sure. Everyone knows everyone around here. Ross was a rich prick, but Dwight was a good guy. He had wonderful stories from his reporter years. You know, he covered Kent State in 1970."

My ears perked up. "I heard he was working on a big story, recently."

"Recently? I don't think so. He was retired for twenty

years or more. Unless…"

I leaned forward. "Unless?"

"There was a dustup about the water supply," he said. "It was a little Flint, a little Dakota Pipeline thing. Something like that, although I could be wrong. Maybe it was just about the water delivery to the rec center?"

Water supply. That could be big. Big money. And big corporations would do big things to protect their big money. It was a lead. Finally, a clue.

We were interrupted by raucous laughter by the fence. The man I was talking with went over to see what it was about. I followed him and saw a number of people playing with a squirrel. The animal was doing viral video-worthy tricks for gifts of crumbs of bread and small pieces of French fries.

"But reverse mortgages are a complete travesty," I heard someone say. "You've spent your whole life working, and you need to get the real value out of your house. That's where I come in."

At the sound of the voice, I froze. I recognized the fevered, manic pitch. It was the second biggest shark in town. John Wayne, AKA Hitler Mustache Face. I stepped behind a large retiree to hide, and spied on the shark as he worked the wake, selling his scam to buy out Apple Serenity Village's citizens, making them homeless and destitute. I wanted to jump on his back, strangle him, and poke his eyes out.

He was making the rounds, and when he turned, he spotted me watching him. It was his turn to freeze. Then, a slow, menacing grin grew on his face. Rightfully, he didn't think of me as a threat, and he figured he could ignore me. He moved on to the next dupe, giving his attention to the group that was playing with the talented squirrel.

A bell went off in my brain. If Serenity Village was in the shark's sights, what if he had tried to work his scam on Mr. Foyle and Mr. Tracy, too? And what if they pushed back, not only refusing his offers, but threatening to shine a light on his shenanigans? Of course, I reasoned, Dwight Foyle's exposé might have had nothing to do with water but everything to do with John Wayne.

Lucy tapped me on the shoulder, making me jump. "That was torture," she said.

"What was torture?"

"My tête-à-tête with Leslie. Did you know that Benjamin Franklin invented the lightning rod?"

Yes. Even I knew that, and I didn't know anything. "What did he tell you about the two you-know-who's?"

"Exciting stuff, like they used to play a marathon poker game every week, which dragged on and on. Nickels, dimes, and quarters. They had a dedicated table for it in a side room here."

"Here?"

Lucy nodded. "Yes. What have you been doing? You've got that look, again."

I tried to hide my look, but it was no use. I had my mystery antennae up, and for the first time, a solid suspect. A suspect that I suspected of killing Mr. Foyle and Mr. Tracy. I just had to figure out how he did it.

"See that man over there?" I asked, pointing at John Wayne.

"The man with the Hitler mustache?"

He was really playing up the crowd, taking photos of people with the squirrel. Then, he turned the phone on himself. Crouching down, he got into selfie position with his arm outstretched. Unfortunately for him, but fortunately for humanity, he had turned the flash on, and when he took the picture, it turned out that the docile, fan-favorite squirrel freaked the shit out.

The squirrel screeched like a cat and headed for shelter, which in this case was John Wayne's pants leg. The squirrel didn't stop until he reached the corrupt attorney's family jewels, and then it was John Wayne's turn to screech like a cat.

He was in good shape for a lawyer and managed to

jump on a nearby table in a single leap, where he shook his leg wildly. The movement seemed to enrage the squirrel even more, and it was obvious the moment the rodent decided to take a bite out of John Wayne's package.

Lucy slapped her forehead. "Oh, darlin', I completely forgot," she said, turning to me. "I have to meet Uncle Harry. You want me to drop you off?"

"No, it's okay. I don't want to make you late," I said.

"This was fun. I wish it had been a little more exciting, though."

John Wayne swatted at his crotch and threw himself on his back, where he writhed in agony, or like he was doing the backstroke in the Olympics. By the look of his frenetic limbs, he was going to win the gold.

Lucy gave me a kiss on the cheek and worked her way through the crowd, which had increased exponentially, as the tavern customers came outside to see who was being killed. I was never a big believer in karma, but watching John Wayne unzip his pants to get at the crazed squirrel was making me believe.

CHAPTER 14

Let's stop kibitzing around, bubeleh. Time to get serious. Sometimes, you're going to find yourself in a difficult situation. Your matches want different things that aren't good for them. You won't know what to do. Don't guess! When you're disoriented and don't know which way is up, take a big step back and rest. Yes, I said, rest. It's not wasted time. Believe me, I matched Stinky Ralph with Cross-Eyed Betty after a two-hour nap. That was a stroke of genius that needed a rested brain to make happen. Rest.

Lesson 88, Matchmaking Advice from Your
Grandma Zelda

It was hard to get out of the Village Tavern because the crowd was thick, especially once the paramedics showed up to give emergency medical care to John Wayne's testicles. As I struggled toward the exit, I was pushed by the crowd into a side room. There, I found others who were hiding from the chaos and not letting it interfere with their drinking. I also saw the poker game that Lucy had told me about. There was a table in the side room with four chairs. A green cloth was draped over it.

There was a sign on the cloth, which warned not to mess with the unfinished poker game.

The bartender was wiping down tables and saw me looking at the sign. "It's a shame about the game," he said. "I liked seeing the old guys every week."

"Is it normal to have a continuing poker game?" I asked.

"It was all for fun. Just nickels, dimes, and quarters. Really, I think they just wanted to be social. The rest of the week, I kept guard on the table and made sure no one messed with the cards. And I put the pot in my safe every week. There's no more than fifty dollars in coins in it, but the guys like to make a big deal about the game. The safe made it real official. Kind of like Vegas."

"What's going to happen now?"

"I heard Leslie and Ben are going to finish the game tomorrow afternoon in respect for Ross and Dwight. Did you know them?"

"Yes," I said. At least, I was beginning to think that I knew them, and more than ever, I wanted to get justice for them.

John Wayne was going to go down for the murders, if it was the last thing I did.

Outside, I called Bridget to see if she could pick me up. "The whole town is an atrocity," she yelled into the phone when she answered. I could barely hear her with the noise on my side and the noise on her side.

"What's happening there?" I asked.

"Justice, Gladie. Justice."

That could mean anything, but I was glad that Bridget had found her groove, again, and was standing up for the little man or woman, or in this case, amateur actors. "That's good. I was wondering if I could stay with you tonight and if you could pick me up now."

"Oh, great," she said, excitedly. "We can order pizza and watch Central Park Five, again. But I'm tied up here for another couple hours. Can you meet me at home, later?"

That's when I downloaded the Uber app and got a free ride. Five minutes later, a blue Toyota Corolla picked me up. It was the easiest way to get a lift that I had ever experienced. It made me wonder again if I really needed Ruth's car. I sat in the back seat and gave the driver the address to the office of the second biggest shark in town. I had a plan to get past his secretary and search his files. It would take every bit of acting ability I had, but I was highly motivated. Bridget wanted justice for the town, and I wanted justice for Mr. Foyle and Mr. Tracy.

"Hey, haven't I seen you in town?" the driver asked me when he picked me up. He was a good-looking man in his twenties.

"Maybe. I'm Gladie Burger. I work with my grandmother, Zelda, the matchmaker."

"No, that's not it. Oh, I know," he said, snapping his fingers. He began to drive away from the tavern. "You used to drive a Cutlass Supreme with big rust patches. The car that blew up in the meth explosion a couple weeks back. Took a bunch of cop cars with it, too, right?"

"That's right." I guessed it was my destiny to be infamous. I didn't even need a Twitter account. I had already been in enough explosions, fires, and found enough dead people to be known forever in the small town.

"Cool, a celebrity in my car," he said. He was very friendly and didn't seem scared at all by driving around someone who had blown up multiple cars. "Do you mind if I make a quick stop at the bank on the way? I'll only be a minute."

"Sure. No problem," I told the driver. He parked in the bank parking lot and left the car, just as my phone rang. It was Lucy. "Gladie, I got the translation of the shorthand. I'm emailing it over."

I put her on speaker and checked my email. I read the translation, but I wasn't sure I was reading it right. "Holy moly. Is this…?"

"A detailed list of Mr. Foyle's bowel movements? Yes, it is. He was very constipated, as you can see, except when he ate Thai food, which went through him like ex-lax. So, I guess we're not any closer to figuring out what he was investigating."

To be honest, I didn't care. I had moved on from worrying about Mr. Foyle's story, and was firmly focused on John Wayne.

"I got to go, darlin'," Lucy said. "Uncle Harry's taking me out dancing tonight, and I have to get ready."

I couldn't imagine Uncle Harry dancing. He was a short man with no neck and no obvious signs of rhythm or grace. I hung up the phone and put it back in my purse. I looked out the window for the driver. He had been in the bank for longer than he promised. Then, just as I had grown impatient, the front door of the bank opened, and my driver ran out. He was holding a bag, and he was wearing a ski mask.

"Uh…" I said.

He opened the car door and started the motor. Peeling out of the parking lot, he ripped the ski mask off his head and tossed it on the floor. "Thanks for waiting," he said. "That took a little longer than I expected."

A bad feeling, like that my driver had just robbed a bank, creeped up and down my spine. "You didn't. Nah, you couldn't have. Did you?" I asked. We drove a couple of blocks before the sound of sirens came from behind us. I turned around. Yep, we were being followed by three police cars. "I'm pretty sure I'd like to get off here."

"We're almost to your destination," he said. "I don't want to leave you stranded."

"That's okay. I need the exercise. I eat a lot of crap."

"It looks like they're gaining on me," he said, calmly, looking in the rearview mirror. I wondered if there was going to be a shootout. Just in case, I took my seatbelt off and slinked down to the floor.

"It's a small town," I explained covering my head with my hands. "Word gets around. Have you done this before?"

"Robbing a bank? No, this is the first time. I got a good haul. I'm going to pay off the car with it."

The sirens got louder, and the driver drove faster. "At least you got out of the bank with the money," I told him from the floor. "In the movies, they put exploding ink in it. Makes it worthless."

"You think they gave me exploding ink?" he asked.

"I don't know. You could check."

The car swerved slightly, as the driver searched the bag. Then, there was a small explosion in the front seat and red ink sprayed the windshield. The driver slammed on his brakes, and we came to a stop a few seconds later.

It was the end of my first ride in an Uber.

The driver's door was opened by the cops, and he was dragged out with screams of "Police" and "Hands up" and "You're under arrest." There was a lot of noise and doors slamming. I felt sort of sorry for the driver. He was a nice guy, except for the bank robbing thing. After a few minutes, I thought they weren't going to find me, and I was more than happy to just lie there on the floor without anyone noticing.

But the back door finally opened, and Spencer's head peeked in. "Are you kidding me?"

Surprisingly, Spencer wasn't upset at me. Since I hadn't been investigating the murder, he didn't mind that I had been involved in a bank robbery.

"Where are we going?" I asked Spencer, as he drove me away from the scene of the crime.

"To my place."

His place. The place with his bed. The place where he

got naked every night and took a shower and went to bed. The place filled with his naked energy.

Naked Spencer.

Head to toe naked Spencer.

Naked Spencer on top of me.

On top of naked me.

"I have to meet Bridget in a couple hours," I said, remembering.

"Why? So that you can eat pizza, watch true crime documentaries, and sound off on the injustices of the world?"

We turned onto his street, and Spencer parked in front of his apartment building. "There's no mystery about me, is there?" I said.

"Oh, Pinky. You're all mystery."

Spencer took my hand on the sidewalk, and we walked into his apartment building. He bypassed his mailbox and went right for the stairs. We climbed two flights, and he unlocked his door, letting me enter first.

His place was a lot like him. Urban sophistication.

Designer. There was a lot of chrome and leather. The only thing that wasn't cool class was his collection of baseball memorabilia. His favorite Padres baseball shirt had been tossed on a black leather chair. There was a large television over his mantel and on either side, he had bookshelves filled with books.

"Spencer, you have books," I said, surprised.

He took his jacket off and draped it carefully over a kitchen chair. "I have books," he agreed.

"Are they a designer thing, or have you read them?"

"I don't want to blow your opinion of me, Pinky, but I learned to read in kindergarten."

I looked closer at the books. One-quarter of them were about baseball, another quarter were about law enforcement, and the rest were history books. I picked one up about the Revolutionary War.

"I met someone today who used to be an American history teacher," I said.

"Is that so?" Spencer had come up behind me. He slipped his arms around my waist and pulled me close. He trailed light kisses along my neck, and I bent it to give him more access. "Would you like to sit with me on the couch?"

I gurgled, unable to respond. We walked to the couch with his arm around me. He was a big man, and I was small, sitting next to him. His chest pushed at the buttons of his shirt. Filled with a terrible need, I reached over and touched him, laying my palm flat on his chest. He was hard. Real. We had had a rocky relationship, to say the least, but now we were getting real, fast. But I didn't want to start off our romance like this, crammed within two hours between a bank robbery and watching true crime with Bridget.

I figured that Spencer wanted to get things started with a bang, but he surprised me by displaying an out-of-character level of patience. He put his hand on my thigh and caressed it, gently.

"So," he said.

"So."

"I hear that Bridget is planning some kind of riot on Main Street."

"Bridget doesn't riot. She protests."

"I already told her to quiet down, but she hugged me, like she was thrilled to death that she was being told off by the police."

"That sounds about right," I said. His hand continued to caress my thigh, slipping between my legs and creeping up to the place of no return.

"You want a root beer?" he asked.

I really wanted a root beer. The fish and chips had been salty, and it had been hot, lying on the floor of the car, but I didn't want Spencer to get up. I didn't want him to break our contact. I wanted this moment to last forever, or at least until I had to pee real bad.

"You've been having some bad luck with cars, lately," Spencer said.

I almost spilled the beans about Ruth's car. After the dog shooting, getting hit by a bus, and the bank robbery, I had finally come to the conclusion that I would do anything to get Ruth's car. Anything. But Spencer would not approve of me sticking my nose into his investigation, so I managed to keep it secret, there on the couch, our thighs touching, his arm around me, his breath blowing on my skin with every word he spoke.

"This is nice," I said.

"Two hours?" he asked.

"I think we're down to an hour, actually."

Spencer stood, walked to the other side of the room, and leaned against the wall. "What are you doing?" I asked.

"It's safer over here. I want to do this right. I want to spend the whole night with you. Blow your mind. And blow your other parts."

"That sounds good."

"Yes, it does." Spencer was crazy good-looking. When he was around, it was hard for me not to look at him. Now, he was mine, and I could look at him as much as I wanted.

"It's probably good that we're waiting," I said. "I still have dead men cooties on me."

Spencer arched an eyebrow and smirked his smirk, which wasn't annoying anymore. "We could wash those off in the shower together." His voice was deep and smooth as velvet. I had failed chemistry class in high school, but I didn't need to get an A to understand that there was a monumental chemical reaction happening. His seductive words hung in the air between us, growing into something bigger, something that couldn't be resisted.

"I think I'll take that root beer, now," I breathed.

"Me, too." Spencer hopped to it. He flung himself from the wall like it was lava, and quick-stepped to the refrigerator. I got up from the couch and followed him. Handing me a can, we downed our drinks together.

He slammed his empty can down on the counter. "Funny thing about those murders," he said.

"What did you say?"

"The murders. I have something funny to tell you."

"You're going to talk to *me* about the murders?" Spencer

never talked to me about murders. He always drew a line between police business and Gladie business. Sure, I always crossed that line, but this was the first time that he crossed it for me.

Spencer got another root beer can out of the refrigerator and popped the top. "Work with me, here, would you? I need a distraction. I'm about to rip your clothes off and take you on the counter."

"You are? Hand me another root beer." He opened the fridge. "So, you're sure they were murdered?" I asked. It was bad news for Sarah and Naomi. They would be the number one murder suspects.

"Yes."

"They finished the autopsy in one day?" I asked.

"Pinky, let a man speak, would you?"

I put my hand on my hip. "You don't have to get all Conan the Barbarian on me."

Spencer put his can down and grabbed me, pulling me in until there was no space between us. I could feel his desire pushing through his Armani slacks. "Do you like it when I'm Conan? You want me to be Conan again?" he asked.

I so wanted him to be Conan. I wanted him to take off his shirt, swing a sword, and take me on a rock. "No," I lied. "I thought we were cooling this down."

Spencer let me go. "I'm going to have the worst case of blue balls," he complained and took a deep breath. "No, they didn't do the autopsy. But get this, and you're never going to believe this, because I didn't believe this. I made them repeat it four times to me on the phone."

"Hurry up!"

"Okay. Okay. They took off their clothes to process them, and they sniffed their underpants," he said.

I put my hand up. "Wait a minute. They sniffed their underpants?"

"Law enforcement is tough work, Pinky."

"But sniffing?"

"So, they sniffed their underpants, and something was off about them," he continued, ignoring me.

"I bet something was off about them."

"Are you going to let me talk?"

"Yes," I said, batting my eyes and giving him my most innocent look.

"Methadone."

"What?" I asked.

"Get this, Pinky. Their underpants had been soaked in methadone."

"What's methadone?"

"It's a prescription opioid, used to get junkies off of heroin. They overdosed."

CHAPTER 15

In general, people are meshuga. You think you've seen it all and nothing will shock you, and then you see something new, and you're shocked, again. Dolly, I'm shocked every day.

Lesson 109, Matchmaking Advice from Your Grandma Zelda

Death by underpants.

It was a lot.

"I'm confused," I said.

"Right? It looks like Foyle and Tracy were freaky drug users. They soaked up methadone through their underwear. I think it gave them a longer high, but they must have soaked their Fruit of the Looms a little too long or maybe there was a condensed patch on their anuses. We don't have that information, yet."

"A condensed patch on their anuses?"

Spencer nodded. "It's a crazy-ass world out there, Pinky."

"Wait a second. You said it was murder."

"Technically. Whoever gave them the methadone is a murderer," he said. "Pinky, what just happened with your face?"

I wiped my cheek. "Did I get something on it?"

"Yes, your Miss Marple face is back."

I shrugged. "I can't help it. It's like wearing methadone underpants."

Spencer sighed. "You know what? I give up. I recognize a hopeless case when I see one, but would you try to be careful?"

"I'm always careful."

Spencer's mouth opened, and his eyes grew wide, raising his eyebrows almost to his hairline. He exploded into laughter. Slapping his thigh, he was nearly having convulsions. "Careful..." he laughed. "Pinky's careful..." he gasped, trying to get air, but he was laughing too much.

I arrived at Bridget's townhouse before she did. Using the key that she had given me, I opened the door. I waved at Spencer, who had dropped me off, and he honked twice and drove away.

Spencer and I had heaps of unfinished business to take care of. It made me feel both giddy with anticipation and nervous as hell. I didn't want to start whatever we were to each other when my feet weren't on the ground, and right now I was flying at fifty-thousand feet without a net.

Bridget's townhouse was three small floors. The bottom floor was now filled with baby supplies. She had enough gear for five babies. At least I thought so. I didn't know a lot about them.

I walked up a flight to her kitchen and living room. I called up the pizza place and ordered a pizza and garlic bread. Then, I turned on the television. The Brady Bunch was on. Sitting on Bridget's couch with my feet up on her coffee table, I felt the most relaxed I had felt in two days. It was the sanctuary of good friends, where there was never pressure or anxiety.

Bridget arrived a couple minutes later and sat next to me on the couch. "What a day," she said. "I'm totally behind on my bookkeeping clients, but it's worth it. Tomorrow is going to be epic. The whole town will finally know the truth about its sordid provenance."

"Be careful," I warned her. "The fuzz is on to you. Spencer said you were planning a riot."

Bridget's face brightened. "He did? Wow, we're really making waves. This is great."

"You want to make some more waves after dinner?" I asked.

After dinner, Bridget and I dressed in black, and she drove us to the Apple Serenity Village. I told her all about the old men's underpants, and she was ready to help me do some sleuthing, even though her passion was for a different kind of justice. I used my new lock-picking skill to break back into Mr. Foyle's house. "We're looking for drugs," I whispered to Bridget.

We searched his bathroom and kitchen, but we only

found the usual prescriptions. Nothing for opioid addiction. "They must have had a dealer," I said.

"You know, Gladie. The pharmaceutical companies are the devastators of our society. They're supposed to do good, but they price gouge so that low-income people can't afford their drugs. Maybe I should make fliers and go door to door in Serenity Village to draft a group to protest."

I gave Bridget a hug. "I love you," I said. "Now, where are we going to find a methadone dealer?"

There was a *boom* noise from upstairs, the sound that came from the bass in loud music. I looked up. "I might have found the dealer," I said.

Bridget and I left the house and climbed the outside stairs to the two potheads' granny flat. The music was louder there. My hand was poised in mid-air, ready but nervous to knock on the door.

"I've got my pepper spray ready," Bridget told me.

With that added courage, I knocked. The ex-heroin junkie Moe answered.

"Hey, how's it going?" he asked.

"Just fine. I had a couple more questions."

"You want to come in?"

"Sure," I said, even though Bridget was pulling me by the back of my shirt. It must have been her maternal instinct kicking in, but danger or no danger, I couldn't stop myself from snooping.

Inside, Lenny was at his desk, working on his computer. He turned the music off when he saw us. Both men were still wearing board shorts and muscle-T's. "Are you here to party?" Lenny asked, confused.

"Uh, no," I said. "I had a question."

"We heard about Dwight," Moe said. "Total drag. Do you know what's happening with his house? We're paid up for another week."

"I haven't heard anything. I'm sorry. But speaking of Dwight, did you know if…" How would I put it? Did Dwight like to drug his underpants? Are the senior citizens of Apple Serenity Village a bunch a freako apparel junkies? Are you Methadone dealers. "Did you know if he took drugs? Maybe had a dealer?"

"He took handfuls," Lenny said. He counted on his fingers. "Arthritis, high blood pressure, high cholesterol. He was popping pills all the time."

"Not that amateur stuff," Bridget said. "We're talking the hard stuff."

"Jack Daniels?" Moe asked.

"No. Methadone," I said.

"No shit. Really?" Lenny asked.

"What's she saying?" Moe asked Lenny. "Old man Dwight was a junkie?"

"Where would he have gotten methadone?" I asked.

"Nobody deals methadone," Moe said. "I'm the only one I know who has any."

Bridget and I grabbed each other's hands at the same time, and we locked eyes. We shared a silent communication that I understood completely. The only place they could have found the methadone was right over Mr. Foyle's head, and now we were standing in the den of the murderers.

"I'll show you," Lenny said, smiling.

"You want some cream soda?" Moe offered. They were very nice young men, and it was hard to believe they were feeding their landlord's habit. But stranger things were known to happen.

"Moe hasn't used his in months. Isn't that right, Moe?" Lenny asked, as he went through his desk.

"Back in June," Moe said. "That's when old man Dwight gave me the ham to celebrate."

"That's right," Lenny said, still searching the drawers.

"After, I put the rest away. It's here somewhere. Oh, I know. It's behind my paper clip collection."

My ears perked up. The matchmaker bell went off in my head, and suddenly, I was sure, just like my grandmother was sure of her matches. "You have a paper clip collection?" I asked.

"Antique one. You want to see?"

He walked to a set of bookshelves, which was covered in assorted crap. He found the paper clips immediately, secured in a Grand Theft Auto box. I remembered back to when Fionnula attacked me at the restaurant, when she told me about her antique paperclip collection and her award-winning Grand Theft Auto habit.

"Lenny, are you single?" I asked.

"Hard to find a wife when I'm working on my thesis all day," he explained, sadly.

"And you didn't kill Mr. Foyle, right? You're not a dealer? Didn't give him the methadone, right?"

"Of course not. See, it's right here behind the paper clips."

But there was nothing there. The bottle of methadone had disappeared.

Bridget and I went down the stairs. We had walked into a dead end. Either Lenny and Moe were lying, and they had given the methadone to Mr. Foyle and Mr. Tracy, or Moe was lying about being off it, or the old men had taken it on their own to feed their habit.

"I understand how Mr. Foyle knew about the methadone," Bridget said. "But I don't get how they got a methadone habit out of nowhere."

"Maybe they were experimenting."

"Experimenting soaking their underpants in methadone?"

"'I don't know," I said. "Maybe they were bored."

"Maybe Lenny and Moe are liars," Bridget said.

"They're pretty stoned to lie that well," I said, but I didn't know if that was the truth or if I just wanted it to be the truth because I was desperate to match Lenny with Fionnula Jericho.

We walked down the driveway, and I heard the sound of hooves approaching. A deer stopped in front of us, illuminated by the street lamps. It stood completely still and stared at us.

"I think I know that deer," I said.

"Ask it what it wants," Bridget urged.

"Shoo," I said.

"Psst! Psst!"

"Did the deer just say something?" Bridget asked.

"Psst! Psst!"

"Shoo," I said a little more forcefully. Then we saw him. It was the deer's companion.

"I have a message for you," he whispered. "From the twins."

"The twins?" I asked.

"You know, the old ladies. They're waiting for you at their house."

Bridget drove us the few blocks to the sisters' house. Sitting in her car in the driveway, we gathered our courage to enter. It didn't look like anyone was home. There wasn't a single light on, and I suspected that the weirdo with the deer was playing a trick on us, or worse.

"This is where those two men died, right?" Bridget

asked.

"Yep."

"I have to pee."

And that settled it. We got out of the car and rang the doorbell. With the light of the moon throwing shadows in the night, it was a lot like Scout standing on Boo Radley's porch. I shivered. Even though I knew that the two men died of an overdose, I still couldn't get past the spooky feeling.

The door opened. "Gladie, is that you?" Naomi asked. I could barely make her out in the dark.

"Yes, and I'm with a friend."

"Sarah, Gladie's here," Naomi said. She opened the door wider, and Bridget and I walked in. I showed Bridget to the bathroom, and while she was peeing, Sarah and Naomi cornered me.

"We killed Mr. Judd," Sarah explained. She was panic-stricken. Absolutely wracked with guilt.

"He was on the couch," Naomi recounted. "Then Sarah and I went into the kitchen, and when we came back, he had disappeared and the portal to hell chair was slashed."

"But that wasn't your fault," I said.

Sarah grabbed my shoulders. "But we played the Ouija,

don't you see? We opened up the portal."

"And now poor Mr. Judd is dead," Naomi said.

"No, he's not," I said. "I saw him today at the tavern. He's totally fine."

"How did he get out of hell?" Sarah asked.

"I don't think he was ever in hell. I think he just left the house when you were in the kitchen. He looked perfectly fine to me."

"Sarah, did you hear that?" Naomi asked her. They hugged each other in relief.

"We need to get rid of that chair," Sarah said.

Bridget came out of the bathroom. "Do I smell banana bread?" she asked.

We each ate two slices of banana bread and glasses of milk with the sisters. "Did you ever hear of Mr. Foyle or Mr. Tracy taking drugs?" I asked them.

"Bad kinds of drugs, not prescriptions," Bridget said.

"You mean ganja? Blotter acid? Serpico 21?" Naomi asked.

"Uh, I don't think so," I said.

"You mean vikes? Crank? Disco biscuits?" Sarah asked.

"Uh, maybe?" I said.

They shook their heads. "Oh, no, of course not. They were clean gentlemen. They never imbibed."

Naomi and Sarah were back to their normal selves and had more or less put the portal to hell behind them by the time we left. They gave me my bag of belongings to take with me. Bridget and I were both exhausted and decided to call it a night. When we got back to her place, I took a hot shower, and went straight to bed on Bridget's sofa bed. I slept like a rock, and thankfully, I didn't dream.

The next morning, I was fully revived. It was going to be a long day. My grandmother called to say the tent was coming off the house today, and we could move back in. It was also the evening of the founder's play, and that meant Bridget's protest would be in full swing.

But before all of that could happen, I had to find out exactly what happened to Mr. Foyle and Mr. Tracy. Bridget got up early to visit a client, and I walked to Tea Time from Bridget's house. There were only a few people in the tea shop, and Ruth was busy wiping down the bar.

"Ruth, I'd like my wink, wink, nudge, nudge," I said. "And make it a double."

It would be my first free latte. I felt like a movie star at Disneyland, getting to cut the line. Ruth made the latte without complaint and put it in a to go cup on the counter. "Here you go," she said. "And here you go," she added, putting her car keys next to the latte.

"What's this?"

"A deal's a deal. I've never welched on a deal, yet, and I'm not starting now."

"But I didn't solve it."

"Spencer came in here this morning, ordered his coffee and told me they OD'd. He also told me that you've been snooping on overtime. So, I guess this is where I say thank you." She blushed when she said the last bit.

"But Ruth, I didn't solve it. The deal was that I had to solve it."

"Don't annoy me, girl," she said, getting visibly annoyed. "My sisters are out of the picture, and that's all I care about."

I leaned forward and lowered my voice "So, Spencer said we're all in the clear, even though we hid the bodies?"

"Yes. I guess the cop isn't so bad, after all."

I pushed the keys over to her. "I don't want the car yet.

I don't deserve it, yet. I haven't solved the murders. But I'm going to work on it this morning."

"Suit yourself," she said, pocketing the keys.

I walked outside with my latte and took a sip. It was the best latte I had ever tasted, maybe because it didn't cost me a penny. Another man stepped out of Tea Time behind me. "Are you Gladie?" he asked. "I'm Frank. Ruth suggested that you might need a ride."

"I'm going to Apple Serenity Village. Are you going in that direction?"

"Yes, hop in. This is me." He pointed to the Honda parked in front of the shop. I got in and put on my seatbelt. Frank started the car and put it into drive but came to a stop after a second. "What's that?" he asked pointing to something in the street.

"Just some litter, I think."

He smiled. "I have a thing about litter. Can't stand it. I'll be right back."

Frank hopped out of the car, ran in front and picked up the litter. Unfortunately, he forgot to put the car into park. Thinking quickly, I did it for him.

But not before it ran over his foot, giving him a spiral fracture. I put the car into reverse, called the paramedics, and helped Frank back into Tea Time. Once he was seated and waiting for medical care, I walked to the bar and slapped my hand on it.

"Fine," I told Ruth. "I give up. I'm never getting a ride from someone else again. Give me my car." She threw the keys up in the air, and I caught them.

"It's gassed up and parked around the corner," she said. "Be sure you're good to it."

I was in heaven. I was the master of my own destiny, the ruler of my land. I was unstoppable, and not just because my car could be mistaken for a tank.

My car.

My car.

It was the car I remembered, the one I had before it blew up, but this one was in perfect shape, like it had just come off the dealer lot. It drove like a dream, and it was all mine. I didn't have to worry about getting shot by a dog, or being an accessory to bank robbers. If I wanted to go somewhere, I only had to hop into my car and go.

I rolled down the windows and turned on the radio. I sipped the coffee while I drove back to Apple Serenity Village.

It was packed with active seniors, walking and golf carting. I parked in front of the tavern and was careful to lock up my car.

There was a closed sign, but I tried the door, anyway, and it opened. Inside, it was completely different than it was the day before. The only soul in the place was the bartender, who greeted me when I entered.

"How can I help you?" he asked.

"I had a couple questions about Dwight Foyle and Ross Tracy."

"Sure. Follow me in back." We walked back to his small office. A desk, chair, safe, and two file cabinets were stuffed into the small room. There was barely enough space for us both to fit. "Turn around," he ordered.

"What?"

"Just while I open the safe." I turned around, and a few seconds later, I heard the safe open and then close. "Coast is clear," he said.

He was holding a baggie, filled with coins. "It's the winnings for the last poker game. They're coming in any minute. How can I help you?"

I focused on the baggie in his hand. Something about it bothered me, but I couldn't think why. I asked the bartender about the two dead men's drug use, but he only knew that they enjoyed a beer when they came into the tavern.

We walked out front, just as Mr. Judd walked in with another man around his age. Mr. Judd was surprised to see me, but smiled and introduced me to his friend.

"Ben Hayashi," the man said, extending his hand. "What are you doing here so early?"

"You probably forgot something?" Mr. Judd asked. "Yesterday was chaos. That man had to have emergency surgery on his privates. Isn't that something?"

"It couldn't have happened to a nicer person," is what I thought, but I said, "Terrible. Just terrible. No, I was just visiting..." I pointed to the bartender. To his credit, he didn't rat me out. For some reason, I didn't want to ask the two old men about their friends' drug habits. Something told me that it was one for all and all for one in their group.

"Help yourself to a cup of coffee from behind the bar while I set them up," the bartender told me and walked with the other men to the side room where the poker game took place.

I took a cup from behind the bar and poured myself some coffee from the coffee maker. The cogs of my brain were still working overtime, trying to figure out what was wrong about the coins. Quietly, I walked across the bar and entered the side room. The bartender had taken the cover off the table and laid the pot of coins in the center. Each man took a handful of coins from their pockets that they had brought from home and put them in front of them. Ben gathered the cards and re-shuffled them.

"Last game," he said.

"Yes, last game," Leslie said.

"I'll get you coffee," the bartender told them and walked past me.

Suddenly, I was hit with a bolt of clarity. That's when I knew that the deaths weren't accidents, that Mr. Foyle and Mr. Tracy were murdered and didn't know they were wearing methadone-soaked underpants, and that someone else was going to die today.

CHAPTER 16

Click! Click, click, click, click, click! No, I'm not taking a picture of you, dolly. No, that's not the arthritis in my knees acting up. I'm talking about clicking. You know what I mean. Match clicking. Love clicking. When it all clicks, it's magic. And what is love but magic clicking? As a matchmaker, your happiest moments happen when it all clicks. In this job, you'll have handfuls of loose ends to tie up, and you'll think that it can't come together, and then....Click! It does.

Lesson 114, Matchmaking Advice from Your
Grandma Zelda

I couldn't figure out how to prove it. I couldn't figure out how to save a life. I couldn't go to Spencer with accusations. If I pointed a finger now, I would be laughed at. But by the time I had proof, another man might be swimming with the fishes. Or wearing fishy underpants.

It was time to get my feet back on the ground and return to my foundation. My support system. My retaining wall. I needed a moment of calm to reflect and figure out a way to prove my theory. Miss Marple would sit in her cottage and knit something.

Why didn't I ever learn how to knit?

Fred was putting the tent away in his truck as I drove up my grandmother's driveway. I waved at him and honked twice. "Look at my car, Fred," I called and then parked.

"Holy smokes, Underwear Girl, you must have a doozy of a mechanic. The last time I saw your car, it was incinerated."

"It's a new car. I sort of bought it from Ruth."

"It's a dilly," he said.

"It has keys, too," I said holding up my keychain. "And the trunk closes."

"That's nice," he said, getting distracted.

"Are you okay, Fred?"

He dropped his head and sighed. "I found an earwig in my pants, Underwear Girl."

"Excuse me?"

"Thank goodness I found it before it made more progress." He shuddered. "It was moving fast. For an earwig, I mean. It was hellbent on getting in my caboose."

"That's rough, Fred."

"There's a lot of bugs in this world. A lot more than I thought."

I patted his back. "Fred, I think it's time to ask Chief Bolton for your job back."

"But..."

"No buts, Fred. You almost had an earwig in your butt. Is that the life you want? Earwigs in your butt?"

Fred shuddered, again. "Oh, no. I don't think that would be a good life."

"There's no bugs at the police station," I pointed out.

His face brightened. "And I was a good desk sergeant, you know. Real good. I kept the desk neat and tidy, and I greeted everyone with a smile."

I wasn't sure how important it was to greet criminals with a smile, but I wanted to see Fred happy again. It wasn't a sure bet that Spencer would give him his job, back, though. He had seemed pretty happy to have gotten rid of poor Fred.

"I'll go over there after work and get my job back," Fred said, suddenly resolute.

"Good."

He wiped his forehead with the back of his hand. "It sure would be great not to deal with ants anymore."

"I'm happy for you, Fred. What about the bed bugs? Are they gone?"

"Oh, yes. I hooked you up with some special sauce," he said, winking. "Don't tell the Chief, though. It might not be a strictly legal poison."

elise sax

In much better spirits, Fred finished packing up. The house's doors and windows were wide open, and I didn't know if it was safe to go inside, yet. So, I walked around to the backyard. Warren Buffet's luxury trailer was still there.

"Dolly, I'm in the house," Grandma called from the back door. "Come on in, and I'll give you breakfast."

I stepped inside. I couldn't smell any poison. "Are you sure it's safe?" I asked her.

"Oh yes. Friends washed all the dishes. I got bagels. You want cream cheese and lox?"

Grandma was wearing a housedress and slippers. I sat back in my chair and breathed in the familiarity and comfort of finally being home. Safe and loved. Could I ever be unhappy while I had those two things?

"You've been through the wars," she said, sitting across from me. I smeared cream cheese on my bagel and opened the package of lox.

"I got a car, though."

"That was nice of Ruth," she said. "Her sister used to babysit me."

"She told me."

My grandmother poured coffee. "So, you have a

276

problem. Loose ends?"

"Yes. Can you help me?"

"I don't do murder, bubeleh. I'm a love lady. How's Fionnula? Did you tell her about Lenny?"

I had almost forgotten about Fionnula, but I needed to deal with her, too, or I would be headed to court. "Not yet. I have to find her. I hope it'll pacify her."

"Love is a powerful drug," Grandma said, biting into her bagel.

Speaking of drugs, I was reminded about the methadone used to murder Mr. Foyle and Mr. Tracy. Time was ticking away, and someone's life was in jeopardy.

Meryl, the blue-haired librarian, walked in. "Zelda, have I got news for you."

"About Bird having video game psychosis?" Grandma asked.

Meryl frowned. "Darn it, Zelda. I ran all the way here. I broke a heel on my oxfords, trying to get here before your radar kicked in. There's no surprising you."

"My radar is pretty strong these days," Zelda agreed.

"My radar isn't strong," I said. "What's up with Bird? Is she okay?"

Meryl got giddy with the prospect of spilling the beans. "Video game psychosis. She's off her nut. She thinks she's in an intergalactic war. You know that her salon is shut, and she went after her pedicurist with a ray gun?"

"A ray gun?" I asked.

"A virtual one, I mean. Anyway, I heard she's getting transferred to West Side Hospital's psych ward. But I think she's happy because she can't be more than a size two, now."

"Wow, video games are rough," I said. It broke my heart to think of Bird's suffering. She was a good woman, always ready to help others in their time of beauty need.

"I'm a little fuzzy about Bird," Grandma said. "But I have a feeling that she won't miss my Monday appointment, and she might not be so worried about her tuchus from now on."

"That'll be good," Meryl said. "Tonight's the founder's play and celebration, and nobody could get their hair done. Bird's diet might take down the town."

"Is the founder's thing a big deal?" I asked.

"Is the founder's thing a big deal?" Meryl repeated, her voice rising. "The founder's celebration is the year's number one event."

That was saying something. Cannes put on back-to-back events all year long. "I thought it was just a play they did."

"And there's food," Meryl said. "And speeches and portable heaters."

I liked food and portable heaters.

"Most of the town will be at the celebration," my grandmother explained. "You'll be able to find your matches there. Fionnula and Lenny."

"How about this one, Zelda," Meryl said. "Did you hear that a squirrel treated John Wayne's shlong like it was a hot dog at a baseball game?"

"I heard that one," I said. Meryl threw me a look that could kill.

The kitchen clock tick-tocked, reminding me that time was running out. Someone was going to get killed, but I couldn't go to Spencer because I couldn't prove it. Snooping wouldn't help. I needed to do some research to prove my point. But how? "Hey Meryl, you're a librarian, right?" I asked.

"Yes. You want a book recommendation?"

"I need information about coins," I said.

"Like doubloons?"

My phone rang, and it was a number I didn't recognize. I put my finger up for Meryl to hold that thought, and I answered the phone.

"Is this the Gladie woman I met in the tavern about an hour ago?" a man asked on the phone.

I stood and walked out of the kitchen. "I think so?" I said as a question. "Who's this?"

"This is Ben Hayashi. I need to talk to you. I know you've been snooping around. I think my life's in danger. Meet me behind the old ladies' house. Come now."

Old ladies could mean a thousand people, but I had a sinking feeling that he was talking about Sarah and Naomi.

"Okay," I said, instantly regretting it. I went back in the kitchen and grabbed my purse. "Gotta go," I said. Walking through the house to the front door, I stumbled on the pink bike that Spencer had given me. It was sitting by the front door, all new and shiny.

"He came by early this morning," my grandmother said, appearing behind me.

"He did?"

"Spencer's a good man. Strong. You could do worse."

I couldn't take my eyes off the bike. Its presence was a message to me: Spencer is thinking about me. Spencer wants me to be happy.

"It's his birthday today," I said.

"Don't worry, dolly. You won't screw it up."

For a second day in a row, it was eighty degrees, as if nature had decided that it was going to cut winter short this year. Fine by me. I loved the sun. I parked my car on Ruth's sisters' driveway, but I didn't bother them. Instead I walked around the house to the back. It didn't take long to find Ben.

He was lying under a tree by the shed, and he had been stabbed to death.

I called Spencer, and he arrived with backup five minutes later. "Obviously, not death by methadone skivvies," Spencer said, looking down at Ben's dead body.

"He didn't have time this go around," I said.

"'He?' You know who did this, Pinky?"

"Yes. I didn't know until I saw the poker game at the tavern, and then I only knew that it was one of the two players."

"What are you talking about?" Spencer asked.

I told him about the running poker game and how the bartender would hold their pot in his safe. "So, they couldn't get to it," I explained.

"Sounds reasonable. So, who's the murderer?"

"The last surviving poker player. Leslie Judd, a retired American history teacher."

I chastised myself for not figuring it out sooner. Mr. Foyle would have told Mr. Judd about his ex-junkie boarder above the garage, and Mr. Judd would have had access to the bottle of methadone. After he soaked his friends' underpants in the narcotic, he let them dry and slipped them back into their homes.

I suspected that I wasn't really a prodigy lock-picker but that Mr. Foyle and Mr. Tracy just had very easy locks to pick. Mr. Judd probably found it as easy as I did, or perhaps he had been given a key.

Then, it was a matter of time to wait for them to drop dead. But when they disappeared, he came looking for them.

"At the time, I didn't think it was strange that he had visited the sisters," I said to Spencer. "He said he wanted to look around at their woodworking. Well, now of course I know he was looking for the bodies. He needed them to show up, you see, so that he could reap the benefits."

"What benefits?" Spencer asked.

"The poker game winnings."

"The nickel, dime, and quarter winnings?"

"One of them—either Mr. Foyle or Mr. Tracy—threw a special coin in that pot. I don't know who. I was going to ask Meryl for help on expensive coins. But anyway, Leslie Judd must have known what it was when he saw it, whereas the rest of them had no idea. You see, Mr. Judd was a retired American history teacher. He would have known about stuff like that. He recognized the coin and he wanted it and was willing to kill for it.

"I'll bet you five dollars that Ben Hayashi suspected something and was in on it, but something happened with their deal. Maybe Ben wanted to spill the beans, or maybe Mr. Judd got even more greedy."

Spencer whistled. "Wow, Pinky. You figured all that out on your own?"

"Pretty good, right?"

"I'll have my men look for him at his house, although I'm sure he's hightailed it out of here."

"I wouldn't be so sure," I said. "I think he's still around, and I think I know where to find him. We just have to wait a few hours."

The Historic District was packed with people. Main

Street was closed to vehicles, and a large stage had been built in the little park. Twinkly lights lit up the shops, sidewalks, and the trees. Meryl was right about the portable heaters and food. There were a bunch of kiosks with all kinds of food, and the portable heaters were welcome, as it grew cool after the sun set.

"Pinky, how do you know he's going to be here? Are you sure you didn't lure me here because you wanted a date?"

"Do I need to lure you?" I asked, but it was nice to be walking hand in hand. If we didn't have to hunt down a craven murderer, we could have eaten corn dogs together in the moonlight. "I know he's going to be here. It would be irresistible for him. He told me four times that he was a retired American history teacher. It is his whole identity. There's no way he would miss the town's biggest historical controversy moment."

Bridget's voice came over the loudspeakers. "Ladies and gentlemen, please prepare to approach the stage. Tonight's performance will take into account the two competing histories of our town. Of course, I'm sure the one about our founder being a racist is the correct one, but you can decide."

I turned to Spencer. "Holy shit, Bridget is compromising. That's a first. You think it's the maternal hormones?"

"Pinky, focus. I don't know what this guy looks like. You have to be on the lookout."

FROM FEAR TO ETERNITY

"We have to get backstage to the actors. I'm sure he'll be one of them."

We started moving through the crowd, slowly, which was heading en masse toward the stage. I recognized a lot of faces. Living with my grandmother put me in the center of the town's life. I had a sense of belonging, kind of like being in a large, extended family. Bathed in the warm feeling, I reached out for Spencer's hand, and he took it, bringing my hand to his lips.

"This is nice," I said.

"You think hunting a murderer is romantic, Pinky?"

"Well, I'm sort of always hunting a murderer, but now there's twinkling lights." I looked up into Spencer's big, blue eyes. He was drop dead gorgeous, the definition of a lady killer. And now he only had eyes for me. How crazy was that?

"Did you hear that?" he asked.

"What?"

"It sounds like someone is mad at you."

"You! You!" It was Fionnula yelling at me, again. She was coming straight for me at a rapid clip, and she was bringing the number one shark with her. "You!"

"Not this, again," Spencer said. "Pull back, lady," he

growled.

"I got this," I said. "Fionnula, I found your man."

She stopped dead in her tracks. "I don't believe you," she spat, but I saw a gleam of hope in her eye.

"He's college educated, and he likes Grand Theft Auto."

Her face relaxed. "What else?"

"He wants a wife. He told me he wants one, but he never gets out because he's studying all the time." And smoking pot, but I chose to omit that piece of information. "And get this. He's got an antique paperclip collection."

"What the hell is that?" Spencer asked. I elbowed him in the side.

Fionnula leaned forward. "He does?" She was almost drooling. I had her in my sights. "What does he look like?"

And then a miracle happened. A miracle on the level of loaves and fishes. An eight-hundred-thousand-dollar miracle.

"Like this is awesome, man," I heard Lenny, but first I smelled him. OG Kush. There was a cloud of it around him, and as he got close, I inhaled hard.

"Good shit," I told Spencer. He arched one of his law enforcement eyebrows.

"Lenny," I said, tugging on his Hawaiian print shirt. He blinked. "Hey, I know you. You're the girl looking into the old man's death. I was just talking about you to one of his friends."

"That must have been Ben Hayashi," I told Spencer.

"Hey, I know you," Moe said, shuffling up to me, smoking a big joint.

"I'm a cop, you know," Spencer said.

Lenny and Moe rocked back on their heels like they were going to bolt.

"He's joking," I yelled. "Joking. He's a jokester." I turned on Spencer. "Don't blow this for me," I hissed. "Lenny, let me introduce you to Fionnula. She's a woman. Fionnula, this is Lenny. He's looking for a wife."

Lenny looked Fionnula up and down. "Cool," he said.

"I'm not that kind of girl. I'm not easy," she warned him. I'll say. She was a pain in the ass and quite possibly crazy. But the love would probably calm her down, not to mention the access to a huge quantity of weed.

"I'm kind of old fashioned," Lenny said. "I have cable." His eyes twinkled, but that might have been because of the marijuana.

"You two should get a place up front before the play

elise sax

starts," I suggested. My evil plan was working. I could feel the connection between them, the mysterious chemistry that made a match.

"When we get married, I'll give up my waitress job, but I'll never give up writing," she said.

"Are we getting corn dogs?" Moe asked.

The three walked away into the crowd, leaving Andy Griffith with Spencer and me. "Another one bites the dust. At least I racked up the billables," he told me.

"A happy ending for everyone," I said.

"You dodge so many bullets that you should be in a circus," Spencer told me, impressed. "They could bill you as the Kevlar Woman. You'll get rich."

"It feels great to have the lawsuit off my back," I said.

Spencer put his arm around me. "Don't get used to it. Another one has to be waiting in the wings."

"That was mean. Take it back."

Spencer lowered his hand and cupped my butt. "Okay. I take it back. Now, point out the underpants killer."

Bridget's voice was on the loudspeaker, again, and this time I was close enough to the stage to see her. I waved wildly. "Look, Bridget's on stage. I know a celebrity," I said to Spencer.

"Doesn't she look great?"

"Ladies and gentlemen and all forty-two genders of the human species," she began. "Thank you for attending. First, let's welcome the tree huggers!"

Bridget started a round of applause. Five people, dressed as trees, walked on stage holding signs that said, "Tree Hater Beware."

Spencer elbowed my side. "Hey, look, Pinky, you're a celebrity. I know a celebrity!"

"Smart ass. One of those tree huggers stole my bike, you know." But since they were all dressed in the same kind of tree costume, I would never find the culprit.

"Some say we were founded by honest pioneers," Bridget continued. Six men dressed as miners marched onto the stage. I stood on my tiptoes, searching for Mr. Judd, but he wasn't there.

"He must be in Jose's camp," I said. "One from the alternative history group."

"Hello, Chief, it's me, Fred." I turned around. Fred was standing in jeans and a jacket, looking frightened. I threw him a smile for courage. It was hard to beg for your job back. I had a lot of experience in that area.

"I know it's you, Fred," Spencer said, annoyed. "I

worked with you for nearly a year, remember?"

"Well, the thing is…" he started.

The play continued with the miners, portrayed as honest, upstanding men, discovering gold in Cannes and creating the town and a boarding house for unwed mothers. Bridget turned on her microphone and interrupted the play. "Of course, the founders were probably responsible for those pregnancies and decided to throw the women away into a home, where they would be stigmatized, relegated to a life of poverty, and probably suffer a terrible death with open sores."

Bridget touched her belly and then nodded to the actors to continue. They shot her looks that ran the gamut from confused to furious. They continued reciting the founding of the town. On the other side of the stage, Jose's group of actors were getting ready to start. I took a few steps forward to get a better look and try to find Mr. Judd.

Behind me, Fred gave Spencer his best pitch about why he should take him back, but Spencer wouldn't hear any of it. "Fred, nothing you can say or do will make me re-hire you. Do you hear me?"

Then, I spotted him. Or more accurately, he spotted me. Leslie Judd was dressed as a miner with a pickaxe thrown over his shoulder, and he only had eyes for me. Angry, vengeful, murderous eyes. His eyes narrowed, like he had decided something. It dawned on me that the hunter had become the hunted. Mr. Judd was a dangerous man, and he was not letting me out of his sight. I turned around to tell Spencer about him, but as I had been looking at Judd, I had walked far into the crowd, away from Spencer. I searched for him among the faces, but I couldn't find him.

"Let's give the original historical players, who might be totally wrong about our past, a big round of applause," Bridget announced into the microphone. The spectators applauded. "And now we have a special treat," Bridget continued. "A look at what experts think is the real story behind the founding of our town."

There were scattered boos as Jose's actors went on stage, but Mr. Judd wasn't with them. The audience began to applaud to offset the boos, and it became a battle between the two groups, clapping and booing. The noise was deafening.

"Spencer!' I called. "He's here! He's getting away!"

But nobody could hear me above the noise. I pushed my way through the crowd to the spot where I had last seen Leslie Judd. It took forever to get there. The actors were trying to put on their show, but the audience was making a horrible racket.

"Power to the people!" Bridget yelled into the microphone, but it wasn't clear which people she was talking about, the audience or the actors. She dropped the mike, literally, and walked off the other side of the stage.

I looked around the area by the stage where Mr. Judd had been standing, but I couldn't find him.

But he found me.

He grabbed my arm hard and began to drag me away. I kicked at him and managed to free myself. He raised his pickaxe in the air and aimed it at me.

I ran blindly. I didn't want to die with a pick axe through my head. Blocked in one direction by the murderer and the crowd and in the other direction by the stage, I chose the stage. I stumbled up the steps on all fours and bumped headlong into Jose.

"What are you doing?" he asked me, surprised. "Get off the stage."

Behind me, Leslie Judd was standing at the bottom of the stairs with his pickaxe. I figured I was safe as long I stayed on the stage in front of witnesses. Mr. Judd had to stay out of sight so he wouldn't be arrested. I looked out into the crowd, trying to find Spencer. The audience had stopped booing and clapping, and were now watching me and waiting for me to do something. I pointed at Mr. Judd.

"He's here! Mining is good!" I shouted. "He's here! I love the founders!"

It was my first acting performance, the one of the few jobs I had never had. It was sort of fun, even though my life was in danger. I pointed at him, again, and the audience surged forward to see what I was pointing at.

"They founded the town of Cannes in the mountains! He's over here!"

Through the crowd, I saw Spencer and Fred run toward me. Spencer ran like a bull with his head down. He was a fearsome sight, full of conviction and brute strength. Fred, on the other hand, ran like he was a toy with a rubber band propeller that you wound up and let go. His arms flapped at his sides, and he raised his knees to his chest when he ran. Spencer pushed people aside on his way to me. "The killer!" I shouted and pointed at Mr. Judd.

Trapped, Mr. Judd ran up the stairs to the stage. "You nosy bitch!" he yelled at me and raised his pickaxe. Fred leaped onto the stage, and in a crazy act of bravery threw himself onto the weapon-wielding murderer. It was an amazing act of acrobatics. Fred must have leaped ten feet into the air to tackle him.

Unfortunately, Mr. Judd took a step to the left, and Fred missed him. The moment that Fred knew he was going to have a terrible fall was obvious. His eyes grew wide, and his arms spun around like propellers.

But he couldn't fight gravity.

Fred fell like a lead balloon. He even seemed to speed

up as he got closer to the stage floor. Then, he landed, and it made a noise like a freight train hitting another freight train. Somehow, he didn't try to brace himself. His hands didn't try to break his fall. Instead, he landed flat on his face.

A perfect ten out of ten for faceplants.

Fred didn't move. He didn't even moan. There was a fifty percent chance he was dead. "Don't be dead, Fred," I said. "Please don't be dead."

Distracted by Fred, I completely forgot that I was about to be murdered with a pickaxe. "Why couldn't you mind your business?" Mr. Judd bellowed.

"I might have a murder problem," I said, and Spencer appeared. He picked me up like a sack of potatoes and placed me out of harm's way.

"Are you okay?" he asked me, his voice strained with worry.

"I think so."

He turned and went after Leslie Judd, like he was a linebacker at the Superbowl. Mr. Judd swung his pickaxe, but Spencer knocked his arm, sending the axe flying behind the stage. Then, Spencer balled up his fist and let fly with an uppercut. Mr. Judd spun around and collapsed in a heap on top of Fred, unconscious.

"Don't fuck with my girl!" Spencer shouted at his prostrate body.

The audience erupted in thunderous applause and shouts of "Bravo! Bravo!" Jose and his actors took a bow. Spencer took my hand, and we bowed, too. The cheers turned to shouts, demanding an encore.

"An encore?" I asked Spencer. "What the hell do they want us to do for an encore?"

"I swear to God, Pinky, if you bring another killer up on this stage, I'll…"

I put my hands on my hips and faced him. "You'll what?"

He grabbed me like it was VJ Day and kissed me for everything he was worth. Then, he let me go and took another bow. The shouts for an encore got louder.

"We're a hit!" I said, thrilled. "I wish we could give them an encore!"

Like an answer to my prayer, Bird Gonzalez, my hairdresser and a video game diet psycho, stormed the stage. She was wearing dirty pants and a t-shirt. Her hair was greasy and a mess, and she was barefoot and desperately needed a pedicure.

But she was rail thin.

"I'm Radan the Horrible," she announced, loudly. The crowd cheered, wildly. Bird seemed to recognize where she was for the first time since she had started her video game diet. Then, she saw me. "Gladie? Is that you? You need a trim. Oh my God, look at my toes."

I gave her a big hug. "Oh, Bird, I'm so glad you're back."

Fred moaned and lifted his head. "Did the bugs get me?" he asked.

CHAPTER 17

My mother ran away to America the week before the worst pogrom in Russian history. She warned her village to get out of there, but nobody listened to her except for my grandmother. My grandmother knew that her daughter had a third eye, and she shouldn't ignore it. There wasn't enough money for her family to leave, but my grandmother gave my mother three silver forks that she had saved for a rainy day. With tearful kisses goodbye, my mother clutched the three silver forks in her hand and went on the adventure of a lifetime. By the time she passed Lady Liberty, she had spent two forks, and her family home in Russia had been burned to the ground, and her parents had been killed. In those days, people didn't expect happy endings, so when she was offered a job washing dishes in a faraway Western town, she thought: It can't be worse than a pogrom. That's how we ended up here, bubeleh. And it taught us a lesson: There really are happy endings. That's probably the most important lesson of all. Happy endings are real. Pass it on, dolly.

Lesson 30, Matchmaking Advice from Your
Grandma Zelda

Fred got his job back before he was wheeled into the ambulance. Spencer said Fred's incompetence was outweighed by his heart, but I knew he was just grateful to Fred to have risked his life for me. Spencer told him to report to work just as soon as he was out of the hospital.

We got a ten-minute ovation while emergency services treated Mr. Judd and Fred. I was later informed that the ovation was a town record. Bridget took the success as a vindication of her efforts toward historical truth. The party continued in the street, but Spencer had other plans. After a quick interrogation of Mr. Judd, he took me home.

"It's now or never," he told me in his car, his voice thick with passion. I didn't have to have my grandmother's third eye to know what he meant by now or never.

"You mean if you don't get it now, you'll never want it?"

"Uh…let me rephrase what I said. I mean to say, it's now, Pinky. Now."

"You won't get an argument out of me." We had had a bumpy road with the start of our relationship. A lot of almosts. Now that the murderer was found, my lawsuit was dropped, I had a car again, and the bed bugs were dead, it was time to settle back and bonk like rabbits.

With the promise of what was to come in the air, we grew quiet, like any words would break the momentum. Or the magic.

It was a short ride home, but it seemed to take forever. Spencer parked behind my Oldsmobile and turned off the car. He took off his seatbelt and without preamble, grabbed me, popping my seatbelt open with the casual ease of a frat boy unhooking his girlfriend's bra.

But there was nothing casual about the way he kissed me. There was conquering in it, like he was planting his flag. And I wanted to be conquered by him. Taken. I wanted that animalistic connection between us. I was sure that that was the only way we could cement whatever we had together. No amount of sweet, butterfly kisses and gentle caresses would be enough to mark this beginning. What had Spencer said? "It was now or never." But I thought he really meant: It was all or nothing.

His lips took mine. His tongue invaded my mouth. It wasn't that he was in control and I was his willing victim, but that he transformed me. Through whatever power he had, I changed. I was no longer Gladie Burger, no longer built of atoms and DNA strands. I was altered, made only of emotion and feeling.

I was so altered, that the fact that I was drowning in Spencer, feeling what I had never felt before, didn't scare me at all. I was exactly where I needed to be, exactly who I needed to be, and exactly with the one I needed to be with.

His hand touched the back of my head and pulled me in closer. My face got hot, my body liquid. Our kiss went on and on, at once both more than I could handle and not nearly enough. I was sure that Spencer felt the same. His hands began to roam, to find my breast, my thigh and then up, up, until I separated my legs and let him touch me for the first time.

Then, he was gone. He broke off the kiss, separated from me, and opened his car door. He walked around the car to my door, and I took deep breaths, trying to come back to myself. It was no use. I was too far gone. He opened my door and pulled me out, bringing me in to him. His arousal pressed against my belly. He held one of my arms, and his other hand reached behind me, under my butt, to pull me even tighter.

Spencer studied my face under the moonlight, as if he was worried that he would forget what it looked like, or as if he was afraid that this would end or it wasn't real.

"I love you, Spencer," I said.

This time, I was aware of what I was saying, and I would remember the moment I said it for the rest of my life.

He groaned and placed his forehead on mine. I could feel his heart race and his attempt to control his breathing. "I love you, Gladys Burger," he whispered, and I believed it. I knew it was true, like nothing else in the world was true.

"Come on," he croaked. Taking my hand, we rushed to the front door of the house. I fumbled in my purse for my key and finally opened the door. Once inside, he pushed me up against the wall. I dropped my purse and threw my arms around his neck. He kissed me again, igniting me into a fiery blaze, and I lifted my leg, curling it slowly around his and making him moan into my mouth. He picked me up, bringing my legs around his hips and turned around to walk upstairs.

But he forgot about the bike. His thoughtful present that my grandmother had left in the entranceway right in front of the stairway.

We went down in stages. Spencer crashed into the pink bike, making the bell ring. He stumbled, off balance because he was carrying me. He fell backward, but fought against it, and for a split second, I thought he was going to win. But he didn't. We went down in a tangle of metal, making the bicycle crash to the floor. Spencer tried to shield me from the worst of it, but there was plenty of pain to go around.

The light on the stairs turned on. "Dolly? Is that you?"

"Yes, Grandma. I'm sorry we bothered you."

Spencer rolled us off the bike, which was now bent and broken. "Sonofabitch," he growled. "Am I ever going to get in your pants!"

My grandmother walked down the stairs and stood over us. "Is this how you're starting this journey together? With your Grandma Zelda upstairs watching *Hart to Hart* reruns?"

She had a point. There was a lot of *ew* factor in being a sex monster when my grandmother was in the other room.

"What's the matter, Spencer? Your place isn't good enough? You forgot to wash the sheets?" she asked.

Spencer punched the floor. "My place! Why didn't I take you to my place?"

"Should I call a doctor?" Grandma asked. "Any broken bones?"

"I think I'm okay," I said.

Grandma nodded. "I thought you'd like to know that the FBI arrested John Wayne in the hospital after the doctors sewed up his pee-pee."

"John Wayne?" Spencer asked, sitting up.

"The second biggest shark in town," I said. "That's great, Grandma. I hope they put him away for years."

"He has to pay back all of the alta-cockers he cheated," she said. "Speaking of arrested, I heard that you found another one."

"Miss Marple bagged another killer," Spencer said. "Craziest case ever."

"I don't understand murder," Grandma said. "Why did he do it?"

"A poker game," I said. "A rare coin, I'm thinking."

"On the nose," Spencer said. "It was a 1913 Liberty Head nickel worth twenty-million-dollars."

"A nickel worth twenty million?" asked Grandma. "Now that's what I call inflation."

"Dwight Foyle played the nickel on Sunday during the game. He thought it was a regular nickel, but Judd was an American history teacher. He recognized it, and Ben Hayashi saw his reaction."

"With the nickel locked up, Judd couldn't get to it. So, he killed Foyle and Tracy," I said. "But he made it look like an accident and gave himself an alibi because he wasn't there when they died."

"But then they disappeared," Spencer continued. "And he panicked."

"He came looking for them at Ruth's sisters' house. He probably looked all over Serenity Village for them. Then, when they showed up, he just had to finish the game. I knew that anyone who would kill twice for something wouldn't share it with another."

"You were right," Spencer said. "He killed Ben and pocketed the nickel."

We locked eyes, and the heat was back between us.

Grandma cleared her throat. "You know, dolly. The trailer isn't going back to Warren Buffett until tomorrow afternoon."

She walked back upstairs and turned off the light. "Trailer?" Spencer asked me.

elise sax

We ran hand-in-hand to the backyard. Spencer threw the door open, and I went inside with him on my heels. I turned on the light, and Spencer slammed the door shut. Our hands flew to each other's clothes, tearing and ripping, freeing our bodies.

We wrapped our arms around each other, feeling every inch for the first time. Spencer spun me around, walking us to the sectional, where he laid me down and him on top of me, knocking the cushions to the floor.

His mouth crashed over mine in a fevered urgency, and I wrapped my legs around his waist, feeling his arousal at the entrance to my core. Our hands manically explored each other, not stopping for a second in our need to know each other.

"Please," I said into his mouth. "I can't wait any longer."

My body throbbed, demanding to be sated. I raised my hips, pushing against his erection. "Just a second. I'm sorry," he said, unwrapping my legs from his body. He got up and took my hand, pulling me up from the couch. He looked for his pants, never letting go of my hand. When he found them, he took a strip of condoms out of the pocket. "I've been waiting for this moment for a very long time," he explained and kissed me again.

My lips were hot and swollen, and the insides of my thighs were wet from my desire. A moan escaped from me.

Spencer's face hardened, like a sign of resolve.

With a swipe of his hand, Spencer knocked everything off the dinette table. Plates, glasses, and napkins went flying. He lifted me up and placed me gently on the table. Lifting my legs to rest on his shoulders, his fingers caressed me, bringing me to the brink, and then two fingers slipped deep inside me. "You're so ready," he said.

Spencer was ready, too. He slipped the condom on himself and entered me slowly until he was nestled deep inside me. I wasn't a virgin, and I had had my share of lovers, but I had never felt anything like having Spencer inside me.

"Is this what it's like to make love with someone you love?" I asked in a whisper.

He began to move ever so slightly, intently focused on me. His face was all hard planes and angles, just like the rest of his body. I put my palm on his wide chest, and moved my hips, matching him thrust for thrust. His rhythm grew faster, his thrusts harder. My eyes closed, and my head dipped back. Spencer's finger touched me as he thrust, and then I melted. I arched my back as I crossed a bridge of intense pleasure toward ecstasy.

My body grew rigid. My mouth opened, and I screamed. Spencer was not far behind me. I felt him explode inside me with a groan. I lay on the table in the drugged-out state after an orgasm. Spencer's breathing was ragged. Carefully, he removed my legs from his shoulders. He picked me up from the table, and I wrapped my legs around his waist again. We were both slick with sweat. Sated but not sated.

He put me down on the couch and lay down next to me. Turning on our sides, I draped my leg over his hip.

"Pinky, how can a woman be so beautiful?" he asked gliding his thumb over my nipple.

"I moisturize," I said, pushing him onto his back. I kissed the length of him from his neck to his toes. He became aroused again, and I took him into my mouth. His fingers combed through my hair, and after a few minutes, he lifted me up and entered me again.

"We should take a shower," I said, sitting naked on the kitchen floor in front of the open refrigerator.

"Another one?" Spencer asked.

"Yes, I really liked the first one."

We had raided the goodies in the fridge, eating a tin of caviar and drinking a bottle of champagne. Spencer was sitting naked on the floor, facing me. He was a sight to see. "I don't know why you put such effort into your clothes because naked is a great look for you," I said.

"Come and sit on my lap," he said.

"I can't see all of your nakedness if I do that."

Spencer crawled over the floor to me. "The caviar was good, but I know what I haven't tasted, yet," he said, smirking his little smirk. He laid me back and put his head between my legs. "Oh," I moaned and grabbed onto the refrigerator door for support while he brought me to climax. As my body convulsed with pleasure, I pulled the refrigerator door hard, and half of the contents came spilling out onto the floor.

After, we did take another shower. Then, Spencer took the blanket off the bed and covered us on the couch, where we laid with our limbs entwined, our faces inches apart. "I could get used to this," he said. "Just lying with you. Looking at you."

"I never figured you for a cuddler, Spencer."

"There's a lot of things you don't know about me, Pinky."

"I guess I'll just have to find them out."

"Take all the time in the world," he said, making me burst with emotion.

I trailed my finger along his lips. "Happy birthday, Spencer," I said.

He smirked his little smirk. "Best damned birthday of

my life."

And he held me in his arms until morning.

THE END

Check out the next installment in the Matchmaker Mysteries, *West Side Gory.*

ABOUT THE AUTHOR

Elise Sax writes hilarious happy endings. She worked as a journalist, mostly in Paris, France for many years but always wanted to write fiction. Finally, she decided to go for her dream and write a novel. She was thrilled when *An Affair to Dismember*, the first in the *Matchmaker Mysteries* series, was sold at auction.

Elise is an overwhelmed single mother of two boys in Southern California. She's an avid traveler, a swing dancer, an occasional piano player, and an online shopping junkie.

Friend her on Facebook: facebook.com/ei.sax.9

FROM FEAR TO ETERNITY

Send her an email: **elisesax@gmail.com**

You can also visit her website: elisesax.com

And sign up for her newsletter to know about new releases and sales: https://bit.ly/2PzAhRx

www.ingramcontent.com/pod-product-compliance
Lightning Source LLC
LaVergne TN
LVHW020342240225
804391LV00023B/399